# THE WRECKING CREW

### A THRILLER

### HUGO N. GERSTL

THIS book is a work of fiction. With the exception of certain anchors of fact, all the characters in this book are the author's creation. As in all novels, much of what occurs in this book originated in the author's imagination. Any similarities to persons living or dead or to events claimed to have occurred are purely coincidental.

# THE
# WRECKING CREW

*A Bloody Good Thriller*

# HUGO N. GERSTL

SAMUEL WACHTMAN'S SONS · DEKEL PUBLISHING HOUSE

# THE WRECKING CREW

**HUGO N. GERSTL**

Copyright © 2016

**Dekel Publishing House**
www.dekelpublishing.com

North American rights by
**Samuel Wachtman's Sons, Inc.**
ISBN 978-1-941905-08-1

All rights reserved. No portion of this book, except for brief review, may be reproduced, stored in a retrieval system, or transmitted in any form or by any means – electronic, mechanical, photocopying, recording, or otherwise – without written permission of the publisher. For information regarding international rights please contact Dekel Publishing House, Israel; for North American rights please contact Samuel Wachtman's Sons, Inc., U.S.A.

**Editors:** Pnina Ophir, Steve Beneš, Dory Morik

*Cover image:*
*Colorful snakes © Choranzin3d*
*Snake on Sign Edge © Linda Bucklin by Dreamstime.com*
*Golf ball @ Designed by Freepik.com*

**Design and typesetting by**

**For information contact:**

**Dekel Publishing House**
P.O. Box 45094, Tel Aviv
6145002, ISRAEL
Tel: +972 3506-3235
Fax: +972 3506-7332
Email: info@dekelpublishing.com

**Samuel Wachtman's Sons, Inc.**
2460 Garden Road, Suite C
Monterey, CA 93940, U.S.A.
Tel: 831 649-0669
Fax: 831 649-8007
Email: samuelwachtman@gmail.com

# *TO*

Maureen and Ben Richards
Jacob S. Lo
Colleen Miller
Dick & Claire Gorman
Barry Dolowich
The late Tom Burns, a fabulous writer and humanitarian who left us all too soon

*And, as always*

**FOR MY LORRAINE**

*By the same author:*

## Fiction

*Arcade*
*Assassin*
*Legacy*
*Against All Odds*
*Billy Jenkins*
*Amazing Grace*
*Scribe*
*Misfire*
*Standoff*

## Nonfiction

*The Politics of Insanity – 2016*
*The Politics of Hate – 2012*
*How to Cut Your Legal Bills In Half*
*The Pets Welcome™ Series*

# *FOREWORD*

## *Two Months Ago – The Middle East*

EIGHT clicks outside the city. Might as well be a thousand miles away. No wind. Quiet except for the night sounds. Rats. Mice. Probably snakes, too. Who cared? Perimeter guards slouched, outside the compound. Bored. Same old same old every night. Even the Black Standard, the *Jihadist* flag attached to a stanchion to the right of the nearest guard, Abu Omar Al-Mosli, drooped forlornly.

Al-Mosli slipped to a sitting position on the ground. His chin had just dropped to his chest. His eyes closed. He'd barely started snoring when he felt his neck caught in a viselike grip and his body roughly pulled to its feet. Before he could even muster a surprised grunt, he felt the cold edge of a curved knife gently drawn across his neck, hardly breaking the skin, and he heard the soft menacing voice in Levant-accented Arabic. "Not a word, *al'abalah, tafahhum?*" As al-Mosli started to choke out an obscenity, the sinister voice continued, "They told me that when you *jihad al'awghad* die in a holy war you each get seventy-two virgins to play with and four-hundred-year orgasms. Maybe, maybe not, *raghead*, but you'll need to have *cojones* to do anything with those ladies, and balls you will not have, *tafahhum*?" The guard stifled a gasp.

Scarcely a moment later, while the attacker kept a chokehold on al-Mosli's neck, the hand holding the knife descended. Two swift strokes and the now-neutered *jihadi* writhed on the ground, moaning in ultimate agony as his assailant departed and moved silently into the darkness.

❧❦

"I thought you were just going to kill him, *muchacho*."

"That was the original plan. But then I thought of a story my martial arts teacher told me one day."

"Bullshit!" his companion retorted genially. "You never had a martial arts lesson in your life! Pajaro Street is in *gringo* Salinas. The only way they'd let you set foot in there is if you were the janitor."

"Lot you know, *Estúpido*. I heard it from the guy who trained us just before we left *los Estados Unidos* for *Ragheadistan*. This famous *sensei* was supposed to give a demonstration of how good he was. Everyone watched wide-eyed as he smashed through wood and did that other shit they all do. Then one of his pupils bragged that his master was so good he could kill a fly on the wing with a single swipe of his hand.

"Everyone bet a ton of money on that, and when all the bets were down, they let a fly out of a little net cage. The fly started buzzing around the grandmaster's head. The old guy let fly with his hand. The buzzing continued and the fly kept circling. The pupil looked down in dismay, watching his money being scooped off the table. 'Why, *sensei*?' he asked. 'How could you have missed? You've done that a hundred times. The fly is not dead at all. He's still flying.'

"'Fly still fly,' the master said. 'But no more fuck.'"

Amid the soft but raucus laughter that followed, the assailant said, "Okay, *hermoso*, one raghead down, forty-nine thousand nine-hundred ninety-nine to go."

*Part One*

## SOMETIMES A GREAT NOTION ...
## JANUARY

*Monterey County, California*

*Tel Aviv, Israel*

# 1

"AMLODIPINE – 5 milligrams; Benazapril – 20 milligrams; Tamsulosin – point 4 milligrams – can't forget that one, otherwise I can't pee." The crepecious right hand pushed down and twisted each plastic lid and an arthritic finger pulled the orange-and-brown capsule out of its container and onto the table. He continued counting out loud to remind himself that he'd not forgotten any of them. "Zetia – 10 milligrams, Crestor – 10 milligrams, shit, they're so fucking expensive maybe I could just cut 'em in half. Allopurinol – 300 milligrams, Simvastatin – 20 milligrams. Christ, maybe if I just took ten of those and left out the Zetia and the Crestor my heart wouldn't know the difference." He got up stiffly, walked over to the fridge and removed a couple of thousand-milligram fish oil capsules. Then over to the kitchen cupboard where he extracted the remainder of his nightly drug habit – two 500-milligram niacin tablets, a prostate complex pill, two vitamin D3 caplets, a baby aspirin, and the all-important glucosamine-chondroitin horse-pill. Just for good measure, because his back was really hurting tonight, he added three ibuprofen tablets.

"These are the fuckin' 'golden years' all right," he mumbled. "the years when I can't afford gold teeth and the years when the pharmacy companies reap gold."

The big wall clock read six. Time for dinner. Tommy "Legs" Aiello reached into the freezer and took out a Banquet frozen chicken pot pie. They'd had 'em on sale at Lucky's last week, four for five dollars. If he ate only one a night, that would last him half a week, but tonight he felt super hungry, so he plucked out a turkey pot pie as well, put both of his entrees onto a flat dish, slit the tops like the directions said, and popped them into the microwave for five minutes. Didn't matter, they were still half-frozen when he took them out. He put them back in and pressed the timer for an additional two minutes.

Forty years ago, things were very different. Tomaso "Tommy Legs" Aiello, then forty-two and at the very top of his game, ruled his family with an iron fist. That family was, beyond a shadow of a doubt, the most feared of all the American Mafia aggregations, so much so that lesser Dons never referred to it by name but only as *Il Famiglia Supremo*. Each week he counted the number of bodies he was responsible for eliminating. Each week, he counted the number of ladies he'd bedded, ladies which Rosa, God rest her soul, never knew about. He'd laughed at the Feds' new, weak sister RICO law, confident that he'd never do a day in the slam. Life was beyond wonderful.

But that was forty years ago.

The still tall, but now stoop-shouldered, "retired" *Capo* shuffled into the TV room of his eight-hundred square foot house. He flipped through the channels on his 19" TV – Erin Clark and Dan Green, the latter with his invariable and boring "Animal Stories" on Channel 8; Anderson Cooper and a bunch of talking heads on CNN, the O'Reilly Factor on Fox News. Useless garbage. He slipped a DVD of *The Godfather* into the player, turned it on, and ensconced himself in the La-Z-Boy lounger to watch his favorite movie for the thousandth time. Within ten minutes he was snoring blissfully.

# PART ONE – CHAPTER 1

Tommy awoke at nine-thirty, rose very slowly, stood until the pain and stiffness subsided somewhat, and went to the bathroom, where he stood for awhile until a few drops made it into the toilet. The rest dribbled onto the floor. Then he found his way to bed.

Life for Tommy "Legs" Aiello, eighty-two, was, in a word, shitty.

Eight years ago Rosa had died. Tommy wasn't around for the funeral. He was still serving his fourteen-year sentence at the U.S. Penitentiary in Allenwood, Pennsylvania, a sentence which was later reduced to eleven years. The Racketeer Influenced and Corrupt Organization law which he'd so cavalierly disdained had bitten him in the ass, hard. Tax evasion was only the smallest part of it.

By the time he got out, *Il Famiglia Supremo* was shattered and scattered, a ghostly shadow of its former self, which had been charitably absorbed into one of the surviving families.

While it was hard for Tommy to maintain his vanity, reduced as he was to a few pairs of cheap slacks or jeans, some shirts, and one or two pullover sweaters, his one unalterable luxury was that once every six weeks he would go down Fremont Street to the CVS and purchase *Just For Men* dark brown hair coloring, original formula. $8.99 plus tax, a dollar more than the CVS brand, but a dollar less than the "new" formula, which didn't last nearly as long.

Tommy "Legs" Aiello had suffered a humiliating embarrassment three months ago. The Feds had discovered an old, long-forgotten crime: Tommy had tried to shake down a "gentleman's club" in Philadelphia. The U.S. Attorney's Office halfheartedly prosecuted him, not because he'd committed any great crime given the litany of his past life, but simply to rub the aged former *Capo's* nose in the dirt. To no one's surprise, he was acquitted after a desultory, lackluster day-and-a-half trial. The embarrassment came when the jury forewoman handwrote a note on the verdict form, "He should not be sent to the Federal penitentiary. He should be sent home to bed."

Still, Tommy's world was not entirely devoid of social life. Every Wednesday morning, he'd meet up with a bunch of Sicilian guys close to his own age in an old cafe on the Wharf, where coffee for the likes of Tommy "Legs" Aiello was seventy-five cents, and that included free refills. They'd spend hours reliving old times, old conquests, and urban legends that had probably never happened, talking about the days when Omertà really meant something, stuff they'd all heard a thousand times before.

Until two months ago, Tommy had attended early Mass every morning at San Carlos Cathedral. Wherever he'd been on the long road of his life, Tommy's faith had never betrayed him and he'd never betrayed his faith. Given his lifestyle, he'd gone to the confession booth often. Very, very often.

One day he slept in late. The clock on the end table adjacent to his bed read 9:30 a.m. Early Mass had probably ended forty-five minutes ago. He recalled that that fancy private school, Santa Cecelia over on Mark Thomas Drive celebrated a ten o'clock Mass once a month and it was open to the public. When he called Information and subsequently the school's office, he learned that the Mass would be held that very day. Tommy "Legs," who'd never been to the campus, showered, dressed hurriedly in his best suit, threadbare though it might be, and called Yellow Cab, the company that gave seniors ten free rides a month.

The campus was gorgeous, more like a small Pennsylvania college than a school for youngsters. By the time Tommy got to the Colonial Spanish-style chapel, it was filled with kids ranging from 4-year-old miniatures to 8th graders. He found a vacant seat at the rear of the chapel, next to a very short nun dressed in blue, who looked to be in her early seventies. Although he'd never met the woman, something about her looked vaguely familiar. Despite her diminutive size and apparent piety, there was an unmistakable aura of "Nobody better fuck with me" about her that hit him like a blow in the solar plexus.

After the Mass was over, Tommy observed that the short nun continued to sit, nodding acknowledgment to numerous adults, teachers and parents who greeted her respectfully. She remained seated, as did he, until the chapel had cleared out, Then she rose slowly to her feet and walked somewhat regally out the door. He followed her for a few moments as she headed to another part of the campus before he called out, as politely as he could, "Sister? Might I have a word with you?"

"Of course," she replied, her voice deeper than he'd thought it would be. "You are a parent? A grandfather perhaps?"

"No, Sister. Simply a first-time visitor. You've got a really lovely campus here. That Priest was so easy to listen to."

"Father Ron? Oh, yes, he's been coming to Cecelia every month for the past few years. Wonderful man. I've never seen anyone relate so well to every age, from the littlest ones to those of our age. He's got his own parish in Aptos, but like all of us, you and me included, he's getting on in years. I imagine he'll be retiring pretty soon."

"A shame, isn't it, Sister. We build up our wisdom and our experience for a whole lifetime and suddenly it's all gone."

"You're retired?" the nun asked.

"Yeah," he said, somewhat sadly. "They put me out to pasture just like they seem to do with anyone when they think you're redundant or expendable."

The woman sighed, but said nothing. They kept walking. "Would you like to come to my office for a cup of coffee?"

"I'd like that, Sister," Tommy said sincerely.

The entrance to the nun's office, actually an office suite, bore a sign over the door, "Sister Maureen, Head of School." Tommy's intuition that she was a powerhouse had not failed him. This minuscule elderly nun, the queen of the whole damned school, invited him to sit in a comfortable chair opposite her. Without so much as a discernible signal an administrative aide brought a tray bearing a silver pot and creamer, two china cups, and an assortment of cookies.

"Nice digs," Tommy said.

She smiled.

"You're Irish?" he ventured.

"Sicilian, born in Chicago."

"Please excuse my saying so, but you look somehow familiar. Do you mind if I ask you your last name?

"Richards."

"Richards? What kind of Sicilian name is that?"

"That's a long story. I was born Mary Margaret Cerone."

"Cerone? You wouldn't by any chance know a John Cerone? Of course he's been dead twenty years and I'm sure you'd never travel in the same circles as he did, but …"

"Jackie the Lackey?"

## PART ONE – CHAPTER 1

Aiello blanched. "You knew him?"

"He was my great uncle!" the nun exclaimed.

"But you're a... a nun."

"Yes. And?"

"Well, uh, that is ..."

"When he wasn't at 'work' he was a damned good man, the most loving and generous person I've ever met. Did you know him?"

Tommy nodded.

"And your name is?"

"Tomaso. Tomaso Aiello."

"Tommy 'Legs'? *Il famiglia supremo*?"

He nodded again.

This time the nun sucked in her breath. She stood to her full four-foot eleven-inch height, walked over to the door to her inner sanctum, and closed it. Returning to her executive chair she said, "I think it's time we had a long, intimate talk *Don* Aiello. I have a feeling we might become very good friends."

# 2

A FEW nights later, after he'd wolfed down the meat loaf, mashed potatoes, and string beans that Meals on Wheels had delivered, Tommy sat down in his La-Z-Boy and surfed the TV channels. CNN, the Republican debates, all personal attacks, nothing about the issues. FOX News the same. At least he could look forward to Jeopardy at seven o'clock. But that was almost an hour away. May as well watch KSBW. Better than nothing. Occasionally those two Mexican guys had some interesting assignments. He never could get them straight, but he was getting better at it. Felix Cortez was the tall, younger one who covered Santa Cruz. The other guy, wider and a bit older, Phil Gomez, covered Salinas and the Monterey Peninsula. He might even learn something by watching.

The camera panned in on Gomez, who stood outside a boxy, 70s-modern three-story white apartment house. The words "Acosta Plaza – the worst place in the Valley?" slid across the bottom of the screen. Tommy punched up the volume. Damn cheap hearing aids. He was saving his few dollars to get a new pair. Medicare didn't cover that expense. "Doesn't look too bad to me," Tommy said to no one in particular.

## PART ONE – CHAPTER 2

"Acosta Plaza," the newscaster opened. "Daylight. Clean streets, green lawns, looks like any other middle class California neighborhood."

The same scene at night. Three police cruisers, red lights flashing, approached a group of young toughs, hands in their jeans, slouching.

"The Norteños got their start in Salinas, the site of John Steinbeck's *East of Eden,* in 1968. Members pay tribute to the *Nuestra Familia.* Their biggest rivals are the Sureños from Southern California. "Today, Norteños have spread as far as Texas. Arms trafficking, assault, auto theft, burglary, drug trafficking, extortion, robbery, and murder. Nice people."

The camera shifted to a frontal view of Soledad Correctional Training Facility. "Soledad State Prison," Gomez continued. "In 1968, Mexican-American inmates of the California state prison system separated into two rival groups, Norteños and Sureños. Norteños aligned themselves with *La Nuestra Familia*, The Southern Latinos affiliated with *La Eme*, the Mexican Mafia."

Tommy Aiello went to the refrigerator, took out a cold can of beer, and returned to watching the TV.

Gomez continued as the camera panned onto a main artery with moderate traffic, bathed in bright sunshine. "Sanborn Road at its intersection with one end of Acosta Plaza. East Salinas is rich in culture: authentic Mexican food, street vendors on every corner. Workers who harvest much of what we eat. But Acosta Plaza in the center of Alisal is also known for violence. The United States averages 32 crimes per square mile per year. Salinas averages 277 crimes per square mile per year. It's much higher in Acosta Plaza."

After three or four commercials, the camera returned to Phil Gomez, standing adjacent to a large field of growing vegetables.

"More than 40% of Acosta Plaza works in the fields. Nine out of ten of this neighborhood's residents speak Spanish at home. Less than five percent of the population goes to college. Less than eight percent consider English their first language."

A slender young man wearing tight jeans and a black Tee-shirt with a red flag, white circle, and whimsical black eagle in the center shuffled by. "Pedro Sanchez, twenty. He's lived in a five hundred square foot one-bedroom apartment with his girlfriend Angie Morales, seventeen, for the past eight months. He's already served time twice. Two of the 'three strikes' the state allows before they put you away for good.

"Angie's brother kicks in two hundred dollars a month toward their $700 rent.

Angie, who works as an attendant at a local Laundromat, left school in the tenth grade and makes minimum wage. She contributes her weekly pay to the pot. Pedro's unemployed. This is Phil Gomez reporting from East Salinas for KSBW Action News 8."

Tommy switched off the TV and closed his eyes. A little nap before Jeopardy wouldn't hurt.

⁂

"So, Babe, how much did you bring home today?"

"Not as much as I'll bring home tomorrow."

"Which means *nada*? Pedro, why can't you get a regular job like everyone else?"

"You really expect me to do that?"

"Wouldn't hurt. We gotta' eat, you know. For that matter anything would be better than nothing."

## PART ONE – CHAPTER 2

"Yeah, but I got a reputation to live up to."

"What 'reputation,' Pedro? More than half the Chicanos in this town who've done time have earned their way into that 'exclusive' group. What's that gotten you?"

"Shut up, bitch," he said. He pulled her roughly toward him. "I don't think you mind that too much," he continued, grabbing one of her breasts. If nothing else, Angie had the most knock-you-on-your-ass rack in the universe. When he started in on her, she was one hot woman. Nothing wrong in that department.

"Stop it! We need to talk," she said sharply.

He drew back in shock.

"Wha -?"

"Not tonight, Pedro. I need to think."

"You ... think?" Her look shot him daggers. "Okay, okay, I'm sorry."

"You better be, motherfucker."

"Did I hear you right? You called me 'motherfucker?'" He drew back as if to slap her.

"Go ahead, Mister *Macho*." She stood there in silent fury.

They'd fought before, many times over the past months. He'd even slapped her once or twice, but this was a different Angie. One with whom he didn't know how to deal.

"Just in case you're wondering, smartass, we have to do some serious planning."

"Girl, stop trippin'. What are you talking about?"

The girl-woman burst out into tears. Now Pedro Sanchez was thoroughly confused. Never the sharpest tool in the shed, he simply had no idea how to handle this side of his explosive *novia*. He waited until she had quieted down.

"All right, all right, I promise I'll start looking for work tomorrow, okay?"

"How many times have I heard that before?"

"You on the rag or something?"

At that, she started crying again. Between sobs, she fired back, "You wish, asshole. Don't you have any fuckin' idea what we need to talk about? Let me give you a hint, numbnuts. What comes after the number eight?"

"What's this, a math test? Nine, bitch."

"Give the man a blue ribbon for brilliance. And what's a five letter word that's spelled p-a-d-r-e?"

"Oh, shit, Angie, are you telling me ....?"

"Yes, Padre Pedro," she said demurely.

"How far along are you?"

"Doesn't matter, does it? Or have you forgotten we're *Catolico*? No abortion."

Pedro Hernandez Sanchez sat down heavily. Gone was the swagger, gone the flaming desire to jump on his woman's bones. He felt nauseous. He looked into the future and saw himself falling into a deep black hole. No more days hanging around the 'hood with the guys. No more nights cruising the Plaza looking for the excitement of the next shooting. *Padre. Papa.* Responsibility.

Life had suddenly turned very shitty.

# 3

"**Dennis O'Brien**? To what do I owe this call, my friend? It's been what, fifteen years?"

"Eight. A few years before your Iranian caper."

"What are you talking about, Irishman?

"Come on, Ezra. The 'good guy' network. I heard you and that deep cover agent in Iran, the one who makes Melania Trump look like Minnie Mouse, got together afterward and you've been sunning your ass on Tel Aviv's best beach since then."

Ezra Caen gazed over at Rachel and gave her arm a loving squeeze. The American FBI agent was certainly right about her. All that beauty and brains to match. It took a woman like that to make him feel he was very much in his prime at fifty. He returned to the call.

Dennis O'Brien truly *was* a good guy. One who should have ended up much higher on the ladder, but who was too nice a man to claw his way over his buddies' backs. As a result, after forty years with the Bureau, he'd reached the pinnacle of his career: Executive Assistant Director, Intelligence Branch.

Middle management. Ezra knew that at sixty-three, with more than half those years in the service of his country, Executive Assistant Director O'Brien couldn't expect to go higher, and it was only two or three years at most, before they'd graciously show him the door.

And while the United States Congress had passed a boatload of laws against age discrimination, when that great and good government decided it was time for you to go, you'd be gone. With a generous retirement, of course, but all the same, it meant being put out to pasture. Next stop, the retirement communities stacked up all over inland Florida from Orlando to just north of Miami. Where you could play golf or bridge or canasta, who the hell even remembered how to play *that* card game – every day of the year. Where it was sunny, sunny, sunny all the time except when the rains never stopped, and where the Florida state bird, the mosquito, chomped happily on every retiree who hadn't bothered to buy enough Deet.

"You still sticking your finger in the cesspool of organized crime, Dennis?"

"Thank God, no," the FBI agent replied. "I got into intelligence a few years after they started to make RICO work. I'm sure you've heard about the organized crime informant fiasco."

"Yeah," the Israeli counterterrorist replied. "The greatest failure in the history of federal law enforcement." The FBI had allowed four innocent men to be convicted of the March 1965 gangland murder of Teddy Deegan in order to protect Vincent Flemmi, an FBI informant. Three of the men were sentenced to death. The fourth got life in prison. Two of the four died in prison after serving almost 30 years. The other two were released after serving 32 and 36 years. In July 2007, a District

Court Judge in Boston found the Bureau had engineered the conviction of the four men using racketeer Joseph Barboza as a false witness. The U.S. Government got whacked with a $100 million damage award to the four defendants.

"May I ask again why you decided to bless this semi-retiree with the honor of your call?"

"One thing I'll say about you, Ezra. You don't mince words. You're the first to call a spade a 'shit shovel.'"

"And you've got a ration of shit on your hands?"

"Fifty thousand rations of shit, and growing every day. The Caliphate of the Islamic State of Iraq and Syria/Levant, ISIS or ISIL depending on the day of the week or the flavor of the politician."

"Tell me something I can't read every day in *Israel Hayom*, Dennis. Last week it was thirty-five dead and two-hundred-and-seventy seriously injured in Brussels. Donald Trump calling for every Muslim to be expelled, for police to cover every Islamic neighborhood in America like ..."

"White on rice," O'Brien supplied. "A southern redneck saying."

"At least the Palestinian-Israeli troubles got knocked off the front page. Every American running for office or wanting to stay in office is parroting how Israel is so precious to them and how they love the brave Israelis who stand between the ragheads and the Christian Holy Land."

At the other end of the line, Agent O'Brien poured himself a shot of Irish whiskey and drank it neat. "Ezra, you know this call's not official."

"Of course it's not."

"Is your line encrypted?"

"Uh-huh. But it's my private line. Not connected anywhere."

"Me neither."

"So you're Hillary Clinton and I'm Colin Powell and that's why we never, ever use our private devices for email or texting, or anything else that might be called a security risk. You need some avuncular advice?"

"Well, I'd like to bounce an idea off you."

"You don't have even one of the three hundred million people in your country you could talk to?"

"Not even my shrink."

"Surely you don't …?"

"Of course not. My ass would be cashiered out of the Bureau so fast… "

"How about we meet some time next week in Brussels or the Caribbean or some out of the way place like that?"

"How about the Sea Executive Suites in ten minutes?"

"You're in Tel Aviv?"

"Yeah. Suite 3180 and I'll have a case of Pellegrino water waiting.

"Tell me one thing," O'Brien said as they overlooked the sugar-sand eastern Mediterranean beach, which, at that moment, was occupied by some of the most incredibly luscious, scantily-clad female bodies he'd ever seen. "In all its international terrorist attacks throughout the Western world, ISIS has never actually attacked Israel. Why?"

"Precisely because the moment they tried, they'd get the living shit kicked out of them and they know the ones who survived would be sunning themselves in Greenland. Ask Al-Qaeda or any Jihadist organization you want whether they'd like to play in our sandbox for awhile and you'll get the same answer from every one of them. Ask the oh-so-moral leaders of Europe who condemn Israel in the U.N. exactly what all their posturing has done to move us off one square meter of the West Bank. Ask Hamas why they've never come through all those tunnels they've built into tiny Israel. The answer's really simple, Dennis. We're not a country you want to fuck with."

"Why am I not the least bit surprised by your answer?" He poured another shot of whiskey, started to hand the bottle to his guest, then pulled it away. "I almost forgot you don't drink anything stronger than that fizz-water."

"It wasn't always that way," Ezra remarked, thinking back to another day a long time ago. After Galit ... "You said you wanted to bounce an idea off me."

"I do, Ezra. I'm on my way out. No," he said, placing his hand on the Israeli's arm, "you don't have to say anything. You know it and I know it. I never really made it to where I thought I'd be one day. I'd like, just one time in this long career, to have a shot at doing something that would truly make the world a better place. And I don't mean that in an altruistic, holier-than-thou way. Just a little something so that some day, years from now, some rookie probationary field agent just coming into the Bureau might say, 'Yeah. It's worth sticking it out. Look what that old fart O'Brien did before he retired.'"

"I'm listening." Ezra stood up, stretched his arms over his head, and walked to the veranda, eyeing the same gorgeous bodies Dennis O'Brien was admiring. "What's your idea, Dennis?"

"We're losing the war with ISIS big time, no matter what we try. Boots on the ground don't work. We didn't learn that lesson in Iraq, we didn't learn it in Afghanistan, we didn't learn it in Vietnam. So we keep using the same tactics that Alexander the Great tried. We've fallen victim to the most famous classic blunder in history. ..."

"Never get involved in a land war in Asia."

"Uh-huh. Air strikes haven't worked. Russia and Turkey got into a pissing contest over the so-called 'No fly zone.' It's only a matter of time before there's a collision that scatters feathers over a thousand mile radius. Worse yet, who are we supposed to support, ISIL or Assad? There's no other option on the horizon. You think the Turks will let the Kurds become heroes? Not a chance."

"Are you here to lecture me or ask my advice?

"I'm sorry, my friend. I just let my mouth run ahead of my brain."

"No offense taken, Dennis. What's your idea?

"Ezra, in my business I've dealt with a lot of Mafia bosses. Not the foot soldiers, the generals. I was on the opposite side for many years, before I moved over to intelligence. I can tell you one thing about every one of them. They got to the top of their professions for a reason. When they got caught, they hired the best lawyers money could buy, and when they got convicted and sent away, not one of them sniveled or begged for mercy, or sacrificed their particular code of honor, omertà. They may have been the bad guys and they were responsible for a lot of bad things, but they took their punishment like real men and sometimes they were very helpful. They were smart and they were shrewd."

"And your point is?"

"They're all in their late seventies or early eighties now. Their day is done. They've been put out to pasture, to slowly rot away until they die. But their minds haven't died. I heard a saying once. 'Old age and treachery will defeat youth and vigor every time.'"

"And your point is?" Caen repeated, but now he was starting to see where this conversation was headed.

"What if, just supposing, these guys could be called out of retirement? What if they were told that what they were doing was so important to the Free World, to Sicily, to Italy, to the Roman Catholic Church, for God's sake, that all their sins, all their convictions would be wiped clean as if they had never been? Complete absolution. They'd be put on a pension for life, say seventy-five thousand a year, tax free. And all they would have to do would be to get rid of some fifty thousand *really* bad guys …"

"ISIL," Ezra said softly. It was not a question, it was a simple statement. "How exactly would they go about it?"

"America's prisons are overcrowded with young Hispanics who have no place to go, whose lives are finished by the time they're nineteen because they did things they shouldn't have done for no reason other than they had *nothing else to do*. No education, no chance at real jobs. They'd always get the shit-end of the stick, no matter how hard they tried. What if the retired *Capos* just happened to recruit them into the anti-ISIL army? And what if *their* records were cleaned up? And maybe they'd even be paid for their good deeds?"

"I get the feeling you want me along for the ride. ..."

"You know the FBI chief and a lot of international higher-ups. Ezra Caen might not talk very much, but when he does the big guys listen. I'm the 'hired help.' People might think my idea's the raving of an old crackpot. On the other hand ..."

Ezra Caen was not unaware of his international reputation. Indeed, there was a time when, but for the luck of the draw he would have been in Dennis O'Brien's place. And who knew? O'Brien's "crackpot" idea just might work.

Two idealists. A sixty-three-year-old American dreamer, a wanna-be-who'd-never-been, and a fifty-year-old Israeli hero known only to a very select handful of people in the world, who, for just a brief moment of glory, had brought the oddest couple in the world, the Israelis and the Iranians, together.

Two thoughtful men sat together in a beautiful suite overlooking one of the finest beaches in the world, talking quietly until long after the sun had gone down. When they were finished talking for the evening, a plan had been set in place.

# 4

―――――――

"Hey, Big Guy, this is Seamus O'Reilly, Northern Highlands Regional High School. I'm calling to find out why you haven't paid your alumni association dues this year?"

The FBI Director laughed so hard his sides hurt. He'd seen the caller-ID as soon as the call came in.

"Yeah, and your New Joisy accent is about as legitimate as a Dutchman. "

"Is this any better," Ezra said, slipping effortlessly into a genuine-sounding Brooklyn inflection and sounding like a cross between the real Bernie Sanders and his Saturday Night Live *doppelgänger* Larry David. He raised his voice, duplicating Sanders' CNN spot in advance of the New York primaries, "I was born in New York City!"

"Uh-huh, and you really *did* live on a Kibbutz for about ten minutes. Is this a crank call?"

"Maybe, maybe not. How busy are you this week?"

"Why?"

"Could we meet for a day or two. A.S.A.P.?"

"Is it urgent, Ezra?"

"Might be. I can come to you."

"The Chinese are trying to carve a little piece of Bhutan for themselves and the Indians are going apeshit. They asked me to come and have a chat with both sides. I'll be in Thimphu in three days if you want to meet me there. Does that work for you?"

"Why not? I've always wanted to see what Shangri-La really looks like."

"Drukair Royal Bhutan Airlines Flight BK-131 is now on its final descent into Paro. Please check to make sure your seatbelts are secure and your seats are in their upright and locked position for landing." As the A319 airbus descended into a long, deep valley, the attendant continued. "If you look out your window, you will see high mountains on all sides. Paro is 7,332 feet above sea level. The mountains surrounding us are more than ten thousand feet higher. Welcome to Bhutan."

The FBI Director shifted his bulk one last time, silently cursing Drukair's one class economy seating. He could barely fit into his front row seat. He felt a hard bump as the airbus slammed onto the runway. Immediately he felt and heard the loud WHOOSH as the thrust reversers kicked in. He recalled reading when he'd Googled Bhutan that Paro's single runway was extraordinarily short, 6,445 feet, and that as late as 2009 only eight pilots had been certified to fly into this extremely challenging airport.

As he descended the ramp, the large man stretched to his full height, dwarfing the other passengers. When he reached the apron leading to the small arrivals lounge, a nondescript middle-aged man, a foot shorter than the emerging passenger, dressed in a *gho* approached him.

"*Kuzoo zangpo La,*" the man said in a soft lilt. "*Gadaybay zhu ga, La?*"

"*Legshom Kaadinchey La,*" The FBI Director remarked. "And that's about all for my Bhutanese. Nice touch, Ezra. I got here a day early. Where are we staying?"

"Gangtey Palace," the Israeli said. "A lot more private than the capital."

Within twenty minutes the hotel's minivan whisked them into the hills above Paro. The hotel, which had been built a hundred years before as a residence for the district governor, truly was spectacular. Its location, on a hill above the town, gave it an unparalleled view of the valley, the airport's flight path, and the high mountains to the west. Despite its imposing exterior, the lodging had only nineteen guest rooms.

After the American had checked into his room and wrapped himself in a *gho,* Caen suggested they sit on the veranda outside the Director's spacious quarters, enjoy the exotic view, and have a drink to relax. Ezra had brought a large bottle of Pellegrino water. His companion selected Irish whiskey from the honor bar.

"You wanted to see me on an urgent matter, Ezra?"

"I did, my friend. Has Dennis mentioned anything to you?"

"No," the Director said. "Why would Dennis be involved?"

"He's the one suggested I might contact you. A week ago he and I met in Tel Aviv and he ran an idea by me. He wasn't sure whether he should even bring it up, but we chewed it over.

The more I thought about it, the more rational it sounded. With everything the Western Powers and the Russians have tried, none of which have done a damned thing to stop ISIL, he asked me what would be lost if I suggested it to you? You're a friend, you're as high up as they go in your law enforcement empire, and why hand the idea over to the CIA, since I know there's no great love lost between your agencies?"

"And you figured I might not listen to my subordinate but I might listen to you?"

"Give the man a cigar."

"I'm listening."

"What's at the top of the FBI's list of things to do, beside the usual political crap?

"ISIS."

"How much are you guys spending on that dirty little war?"

"I could say I have no idea, Ezra."

"Bullshit! You're the head of the Federal Bureau of Investigation and if I can read the D.O.D. figures on Google, you sure as hell know how much."

"Okay, try a few billion here or there."

"Put it into smaller figures a plodder like me can relate to. Fourteen *million* dollars *a day*! And exactly where has it gotten the leader of the free world?"

"A lot of political finger-painting and a country that jumps off the edge of a cliff every time it hears about so much as one person being killed. When that happens in Paris or Brussels, the Donald Trumps of the world go berserk. How does that tie in to why you're here?"

For the next thirty minutes, Ezra Caen repeated almost verbatim what he and Dennis O'Brien had discussed the week before. It became clear to the Director that Ezra was not trying to sell him a bill of goods. He was simply stating facts as he saw them.

"Tell you what," he finally said. "You've had a long flight and you've got a nasty bit of business coming up in the next couple of days. Even when you're not working, the higher-ups are going to want to do a photo op of you climbing up to the Tiger's Nest Lamassery. I suggest we both take a hot stone bath and you can mull over what I just said. Meet me there in ten minutes."

Shortly thereafter, the two men thoroughly enjoyed Bhutan's version of the hot tub. Four wooden, one-person baths stood side by side in the small, semi-closed bath house which overlooked the Paro Valley. A board with holes at one end of each tub separated the bathers from the hot stones. At that time of the day, they had the room to themselves. An attendant using long steel tongs picked red-hot rocks from the bonfire and dropped them into each chamber, which brought the cauldron in that tub to a boil. The heated water coursed through the holes in the board at each man's feet, causing the water around their bodies to heat to a degree where each man held up his right hand, a signal that the water was hot enough. Then the attendant dropped fragrant herbs into each tub. The mint was refreshing and familiar, but the FBI Director caught a whiff of another aroma.

"Isn't that -?"

"Mm-hmm," Caen replied. "Marijuana grows wild in Bhutan. It's normally used for pig food."

The FBI Director said nothing, but closed his eyes and luxuriated in the steaming water that relaxed his every muscle.

After awhile, he started digesting what Ezra had said. Lord knows, they'd tried everything else and nothing seemed to work. One hundred million dollars in seed money. A little more than one week's expenditure. If it failed, it certainly wouldn't break the budget. And if it worked …?

Later that evening, the two men worked out a rough estimate of the math.

"Fifteen 'generals' plus one supreme leader. They're in their late seventies, early eighties, so let's give 'em twenty years at seventy-five thousand per. Twenty-four million. A day-and-a-half's current anti-ISIS budget. How many soldiers d'you think we'd need?"

"Let's be generous," Caen supplied. "Twenty thousand guerilla fighters. We feed, clothe, arm, and shelter them and we deposit three thousand a month in a tax-free account for each of them at home. About eleven days worth of expenditures for each thirty days' work," Ezra continued. "How long do you expect it would take?"

"Better not take more than a year, 'cause if it did everyone from the President down would be screaming for my ass and they'd probably hang me upside down in the middle of D.C., just like they did with Mussolini at the end of World War II."

"An elegant idea."

"What do you mean, Israeli?"

"Simply this. Where'd they hang Mussolini?"

"Italy."

"Anything else you can think of when you think of Italy, my friend?"

"Sure. Venice, Florence, Rome ..."

"You got a lot warmer on that last town. What's the most famous place in Rome?"

"The Colosseum, the Roman Forum ...?"

"I mean *today,* and for the last two thousand years, if you take my hint."

"Pope Francis, the Vatican City."

"Exactly. The great, good, moral United States of America can't be seen to be involved in a shady deal such as Dennis proposed. But if you could somehow funnel that money to our "army" through the *Instituto per le Opere di Religione, t*he Institute for the Works of Religion ..."

The Director of the largest, most powerful investigation agency in the Western world, scratched his head, then smiled broadly. Not to profane the Almighty's Name, but *Holy Shit* ... this whole operation would be funded through the Vatican Bank?"

"As they say in the game that's helped fund the Church for years, *Bingo!* Who better would want to wage war to achieve peace?"

"Ezra?"

"Yes."

"Did anyone ever tell you you're a fricken' genius?"

"Nope. I'm just a plodder."

"Assume I can sell this cockamamie idea of yours …"

"Dennis O'Brien's idea. Give credit where credit is due."

"The devil's in the details. We've got to start planning this like we're really going to war. From the Field Marshal down to the private and everything in between."

"I agree."

"Any way we could 'borrow' you from your agency like the Iranians did a few years back?"

"What do you mean? I'm officially 'retired' and a free agent."

"I'll need two weeks to talk to some of my friends on the Hill and bounce it off them. But if, and it's a very big *if,* I can somehow get this whacko idea approved, can you give me a number where I can reach you at any time so we could set this idea in motion?"

"Of course. Is it O.K. if I bring a couple of friends to join the party?"

*Part Two*

# WELCOME TO THE PARTY
# FEBRUARY – MARCH

# 5

"Let me get this straight, Sister. You sure you want to tell me this? I mean, I'm the last person in the world a Bride of Christ would go to for Confession."

"Tommy, if God knows, and I'm sure He does, it's pretty late in the day for me to go to my grave without telling someone. Long story short, when I was seventeen and had just graduated high school I fell madly in love with a twenty-four-year-old medical student named Ben Richards. 'Gentle Ben' they called him, even back then. He was Sicilian, just like me. His family name was Ricciardi, but they changed it to Richards when they came to the States. You don't have to look at me like that, Tommy. Yes, we did 'sin,' and yes we did plan to get married, and no, I never got pregnant. One night, he went out to a take-out place to bring home a pizza. He never came back."

Aiello sat silently, waiting patiently for her to go on.

"They never found out who murdered him or why. I suppose I could have hated God and hated the whole world, because my life had been shut down, and maybe I did hate for a while. They say 'A young heart cracks but it doesn't break.' But in my case, I found out that was a bunch of horseshit. Even then, I knew there'd never be another man, but even though I felt dead inside, I didn't stop breathing. One day led to another and then another, and before I knew it a year had gone by."

"Never even dated again?"

"Never dated again. It's not that I wasn't asked. Although you'd never know it now, back then I was a reasonably attractive young girl and I had the standard equipment that goes with being a girl. But when I'd had the best there was, I couldn't settle for less. When I was nineteen, I was still confused, but I had a long talk with a wise old priest, long since gone, who reminds me a lot of Father Ron Shirley. He listened a lot more than he talked. After a few months, I found myself feeling very much at peace whenever I was around him. One day, out of the blue, I asked him what he thought about my becoming a nun."

"Just like that?"

"Uh-huh. Would you like some more tea, Tommy?" It was a Saturday morning and they were alone in her office. They'd taken to meeting there each Saturday morning for the past few weeks. Two people who'd been down long, very disparate paths in their lives, but who'd found a quiet, satisfying affinity for one another.

"Maybe we could take a walk around campus instead? I've got to let out some liquid before I take more in."

"Oh, sure. I'll meet you in the corridor in a few minutes."

After he'd returned, they started walking past the chapel and up the hill to the Performing Arts Center.

Sister Maureen continued, "I asked my Great Uncle Jackie what he thought. His life was way different from the Church's teachings, but that didn't stop him from being religious and it didn't make him any less wise. He asked if I was sure that was what I wanted to do. He pointed out candidly that there'd be no husband, no sex, no *bambinos*, and no grandchildren. 'You'd be the only one who came *solo* at family gatherings. You're giving up a lot, you know, honey?' he said.

"'But there was Ben,' I said."

" 'That was two years ago and then some. You sure you want to turn off to life?'"

" 'Maybe it's not turning off to life, Uncle Jack,' I said. 'Maybe it's just turning my life in a different direction.' After that talk, I found my outlook changing. I was almost twenty, neither too young nor too old to apply as a novitiate. I was independent enough that I could always change my mind. God adjusts to people who change their minds. That was a little more than fifty-three years ago."

"1963," Aiello said. "I'd just turned thirty and managed to avoid the draft. By that time, I thought I was quite a hotshot in the family I hung with. I'd married Rosa, but that never stopped me …"

"Naughty boy," she replied, but gently. "I came out of the Dominican Order and felt I had to make something of my life. Something that would somehow reflect on what Ben had wanted to be. Something that would make his life meaningful, if only to God. I took up nursing. For ten years I worked in Hell's Kitchen at every shithole job you can think of, Tommy. I wiped the asses of people who were dying of cancer. I bandaged the heads of men who'd had their eyes shot out. I'm sure you've seen what men can do to other men. I saw the same things, and I can tell you, I became one helluva tough old buzzard by the time I was thirty. 'Mother Courage' was the nicest name they called me. There were others …"

"Why don't we go back to your office, Maureen?" Aiello said. "I've seen enough of the underside of life that I don't feel nauseated by what you're telling me, but it might be an idea to relax a little bit."

"Chill out," as the young people would say today?"

"Yeah, I think so."

※

Their conversation continued the following Saturday morning.

"It's a long way from Hell's Kitchen to Santa Cecelia School," Tommy started.

"No shit, Sherlock. Another of today's wisecracks. Are you offended to hear these words come from the almost virgin lips of a nun?"

" '*Homo sum, humani nihil a me alienum puto.* Nothing human is alien to me.' Terrence, 165 B.C."

"You really are brighter than you look." She smiled. "The current school was started by Dominican Nuns in 1950. The first principal, Mary Dunleavy, died in 1965, after fifteen years at the helm. Sister Bernice O'Donnell took over when Sister Dunleavy died. She recruited me in seventy-five and I've been here ever since. Sister Bernice was quiet, courteous, and appeared to the outside world to be humble and unassuming, but she was the toughest human being I'd ever met. When she shook hands with you, you damn well better believe her hand came away with some of your money, more than you had thought you could ever afford to give, and when this sweet, quiet little lady became upset, even God would've run for cover.

"Shortly after I got there, there were four of us nuns then, Sister Bernice, Sister Jean, Sister Isabel, and me, the Dominican Order decided to close down the school. Sister Bernice took the position, 'Over my dead body.' She asked the three of us whether we'd stand with her. Tommy, there was no way anyone was going to say no to that woman. Without anyone knowing what happened or how fast it happened, the four of us quit the Dominican Order and joined some small Order that nobody else had ever heard of. Rome has never formally recognized us. Then we took the school independent, voted in a Board of Directors, and kept the damn place open."

"Ballsy," Tommy replied.

"That woman had more balls than any ten men. By 2002, Sister Bernice was on the downhill slide. The Board asked me to take over for a year or two at most. That was fourteen years ago. Sister Bernice died in 2008.

"While I can't think of anyone who could duplicate her, I think I learned pretty well from Sister Bernice. Today we've got an endowment of $27 million. I can't even begin to tell you how valuable the property is, but I do know that two families just paid eighteen million dollars cash to build the new math-science center and this place is 100% debt free. But the Board hinted very broadly last year that it's time for me to go. Sister Isabel and I are the last of the four nuns. We're retiring in July, a few months from now. When we're gone there'll be no more nuns left at Santa Cecelia."

"That seems a terrible shame."

"I'm not ready to be put out to pasture yet, but despite all the accolades they're giving me and the 'How will we ever survive without you, Sister Maureen?' the handwriting on the wall is very clear. You know what it's like, Tommy."

"That's for sure. Where does the time go? The year after you came to Santa Cecelia, I was at the top of my game. Time for me to confess?"

"If you want."

"Every week I counted the number of bodies I was responsible for taking out. Every week I counted the number of ladies I'd slept with that Rosa didn't know about. Today I count the number of pills I take every day to keep me going and the number of pennies I save each month so I can eventually buy some cheap dentures which the government doesn't pay for.

"They'd passed RICO, the Racketeer Influenced and Corrupt Organizations law that I thought was a big joke, something designed to show that the Feds were cleaning up the show. I wasn't worried about RICO, first because in the first five years the Feds hadn't gotten a single conviction and second beause we had plenty of Representatives and Senators in the U.S. Congress who were very friendly to us, not to mention those on our payroll in Newark and Albany. I thought RICO was just a passing fad and would be repealed in short order without a single conviction.

"By the time I got out of Allenwood, *Il Famiglia Supremo* was shattered and scattered, a ghostly shadow of its former self, which had been charitably absorbed into one of the surviving families. The remnant of the Family has been thoughtful enough to pay me a pension of twenty-five hundred dollars a month. The Italian Catholic Federation allows me to live rent-free in my less-than palatial eight hundred square foot residence on Elm Avenue. Thank God, Social Security pays me another five hundred and Medicare takes care of most of my healthcare needs, as long as I pay $190 a month for Part B and another $67.80 a month for my Part D prescription drug program."

"Sad, isn't it?" Sister Maureen said. "I don't know about you, but there's still more mountains I want to climb. It's just that no one even thinks what they call 'senior citizens' even have what it takes to climb a tiny little hill."

"Maybe, but you know what, Sister? I've never stopped believing in God and I've never stopped believing that maybe He'd give us one more little hill to climb."

# 6

SANDRA LOMBARDO sat on the front porch of a little bungalow in Seminole Heights, Florida, her home since her husband had died in 2014. She missed him, but she was making do. At 78, she had her health, her friends, her son, Gary, and her book, *Daughter of the King: Growing Up in Gangland*. And she had the memories.

Like the time Frank Sinatra came over to say hello to her father, spilled a champagne bucket of ice in her lap and looked as though he had made a fatal mistake. Or the time her father took her to the Majestic Theatre to see *Carousel*, the hottest ticket on Broadway, and he bought all the seats in front of them so their view was unimpeded. Or the time she went ice skating on the terrace of her family's 19th-floor apartment at the Beresford at 211 Central Park West. Or the time, later, when she made love to Dean Martin six times in one night.

Central to them all, her charmed childhood, the company she kept, her astonishing life, was her father, Meyer Lansky.

She always assumed he was a jukebox salesman because he had shown her a showroom full of Wurlitzers at his office at Emby Distributing Company near Times Square. His group of friends, the men with whom he broke bread most often at Dinty Moore's on West 46th Street, were all her uncles. Family.

There was Uncle Frank Costello, and Uncle Abe Zwillman, the kings of New York and New Jersey. There was Uncle Joe Adonis, and Uncle Willie Moretti. There were her father's closest associates, men with whom he'd bonded as a boy: Uncle Benny and Uncle Charlie. The FBI knew these men as Bugsy Siegel and Lucky Luciano. They said her uncles formed the mafia, what the papers called the National Crime Syndicate, and later Murder Incorporated.

Meyer Lansky sat in the seat of honor at Dinty Moore's, a stoic, well-dressed Jew, husband and father of two boys and a little girl upon whom he doted. When it was time to talk business, Sandra could see it in her father's face. She'd take her cue and go pal around with the hat-check girl, who gave her candies and let her sort mink stoles and topcoats.

Lansky was the architect of the mob, the brains, the little man in the middle, at home with both the Jews and Italians. He'd had a tough upbringing on Manhattan's Lower East Side. He'd teamed up with Siegel in his teens, forming the Bugs and Meyer Mob. The mob ran bootlegging operations and gambling rings. The cops would eventually start investigating them for racketeering, theft, extortion, even murder. The Feds believed the Bugs and Meyer Mob helped Lucky Luciano take control of New York by offing mob kings Joe Masseria, who was found with an ace of spades in his lifeless hand, and Salvatore Maranzano, the "boss of bosses."

For all the tales of bloodshed and bootlegging in the press linked to her father and uncles, Sandra Lansky had a hundred more about how much they loved her. They hugged her, kissed her, cut her steak, and spoiled her rotten.

## PART TWO – CHAPTER 6

For the mascot of the mob, ignorance was bliss. The men she knew were not in the business of murder. They were in business. Casinos and nightclubs, tailored suits and penthouse suites, vacations in Miami Beach and Las Vegas. The rubouts and warfare of their youths seemed to be in the past. They found opportunity in America. As a way of saying thanks, they helped their new country win World War II.

Sandra remembered the day her father took her to view the French luxury liner *Normandie*, which had been sabotaged and was burning on the West Side docks. Then the two of them went to Dinty Moore's, where Lansky met with Uncle Joe, Joseph Lanza, head of the Seafood Workers' Union and one of the most powerful men on the waterfront, to cook up a patriotic plan to secure the docks and root out traitors who might destroy other ships. All in return for freeing Luciano, who had been sent to prison on prostitution charges.

Sandra's first hint that her father might not be what she thought he was came when she was thirteen. She stopped at a newsstand and saw her father's picture on a magazine. She secretly took it home, where she read that her father and uncles were the most powerful criminals in the world.

There was no mention of the money the mob had raised for orphans or the work they did during World War II. According to the magazine, these guys were evil, nothing more.

"But they did a lot of good," the daughter said in an interview, years later. "These guys came to this country with nothing, little education and no opportunity. The boatloads that had come prior to them would beat them up and belittle them on a daily basis. So they just tried to stick together and make money any way they could. At the end of the war, my father received a copy of the signing of the surrender, from the Navy department. He was very proud of that."

But the momentum had shifted. Sandra watched the Kefauver hearings on television in 1951, and saw her uncles nervously testifying before the Tennessee senator and crusader against organized crime. She worried that the Feds would be coming for her father.

"Don't believe any of this stuff," her mother said. "It's all lies."

Meyer Lansky, the man in the middle, was never called to testify. His daughter eventually found out why. Lansky met privately with Kefauver. He knew something few others did. Connections in Hot Springs, Arkansas gave Lansky log books from the race track that showed Kefauver had a gambling problem and had run up debt.

"He went in there and pulled an IOU out of his pocket," Sandra later said. "Kefauver was a big gambler. And that was that."

Even so, Meyer Lanksy had become a household name. But the man who didn't like being recognized still did business at Dinty Moore's. In 1951, her father was talking business with Uncle Willie Moretti when Moretti made an offensive comment. "Willie, you talk too much," Meyer Lansky said. Then he called for the check.

The next day at school, Sandra saw one of the janitors reading the newspaper. There was Uncle Willie in a pool of blood on the floor at Joe's Elbow Room in New Jersey. The headline read, "Mob Boss Exterminated in New Jersey."

Moretti was the second uncle she had lost to bullets. A few years before, someone had gunned down her Uncle Benny "Bugsy" Siegel in Beverly Hills. He was accused of squandering mob money building The Flamingo in Vegas.

## PART TWO – CHAPTER 6

Sandra Lansky bottled her curiosity. Meyer Lansky's daughter knew the key to survival: Never complain, never explain. And never ask to be explained to.

One of the few times she recalled her father explaining his business was in 1953, before he went to jail on gambling charges in upstate New York. He had opted to do sixty days to avoid trial. "He said to me that he had two choices," Sandra said. "He could walk down one road or the other road."

Lansky moved to Florida upon his release. Life didn't get easier for her. The government had cranked up its investigations as the mob's casino ambitions grew. The FBI was watching Meyer Lansky's gambling operations in Las Vegas, South Florida, and Havana, Cuba, where Cuban President General Fulgencio Batista, had rolled out the welcome mat. Lansky invested big in Cuba. Two years later, when the Cuban revolution brought Fidel Castro to power, revolutionaries smashed slot machines and shuttered the casinos.

Meanwhile, more of Sandra's uncles were falling. Someone rubbed out Albert Anastasia in the barbershop of the Park Sheraton Hotel. They said her Uncle Abe had hanged himself in his basement in West Orange. Soon Sandra, who'd given birth to her son, Gary, got caught up in the mess. She befriended a man who turned out to be an FBI spy. She fearfully told her father, who brainstormed a way to use his daughter's new relationship to keep the FBI off his trail. Sandra began feeding the man bad information. She'd been betrayed, but she was a Lansky, and Lansky blood was thick."I got my vendetta," she later said.

In 1964, Sandra married Vince Lombardo, a mobster, who promised her father he'd get out and stay out as long as he was with Sandra. They remained happily married for fifty years, until his death.

The FBI tightened its noose on Meyer Lansky. Agents tracked his every move and overheard him boast that organized crime was "bigger than U.S. Steel." Lansky sought asylum in Israel, but was forced back to Miami. When the plane touched down in November 1972, he was arrested on charges of tax evasion, conspiracy and skimming casino profits, but nothing stuck.

Lansky was celebrated in Miami even if the papers called him Public Enemy Number 1. She remembered getting letters addressed to the "Mayor of Miami Beach."

A heavy smoker all his life, Meyer Lansky died on January 15, 1983, after fighting lung cancer. Forbes had estimated his wealth at $300 million, but there was very little money in the will. His family still wonders where it went. Lansky was buried in Mount Nebo Cemetery in Miami. His daughter visited often, until she relocated to Tampa. Her only connection to Tampa was "Santo," Santo Trafficante Jr., one of the last of the old-time bosses.

She was still mourning her father, thirty-three years later.

In a September 1971 letter, her father wrote to Sandra, "When you lose your money, you lose nothing; when you lose your health, you lose something; when you lose your character, you lose everything."

She was reminiscing about her father for the thousandth time one morning in February 2016 when her son, Gary Rapoport, came onto the porch where she was sitting. "Mom, there's some guy calling from Israel. He says his same is Ezra Caen and he'd like to talk to you if you have a few minutes."

# 7

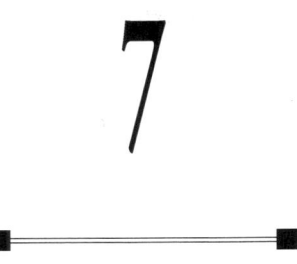

To: Candycaen@netvision.net.il
From: feebee15.dennis@me.com
8:49 a.m.

Papa says game on. Start recruiting.

# 8

CASTELLAMMARE del Golfo, a town of fifteen thousand in the Trapani Province of Sicily, is as magically picturesque as any small coastal commune in Italy. But for the fishing and, most recently, the tourist industry occasioned in large part by its association with the Mafia, it would be dirt poor. Situated between Palermo and Trapani, the small town has been the birthplace of many American Mafia figures, including Salvatore Maranzano, Stefano Magaddino, Vito Bonventre, John Tartamella, and Joseph Bonanno. The Castellamarese war, fought by the Masseria clan against the Maranzano clan for the control of the Italian Mafia in New York City, originated here. Castellammare del Golfo rises at the foot of Mount Inici and gives the name to the surrounding gulf, which stretches from Capo Rama on the east as far as Capo San Vito on the west.

Coming from Palermo, after getting off at the Castellammare railway station, Ezra entered the town and stopped for a refreshing glass of Pellegrino at a small bar on Largo Petrolo, where he enjoyed a wonderful view of the Gulf. He glanced at his watch. One-thirty. He'd arranged to meet Giuseppe Riina at 2:00 at the Town Hall. After a leisurely walk through town, he arrived ten minutes early, just to be on the safe side.

## PART TWO – CHAPTER 8

He'd been walking in the park adjacent to the municipal building for less than two minutes when he felt a presence at his side. Without turning to acknowledge anything, he stated, "Signor Riina?"

"Si. *Shalom*, Signor Caen." Ezra smiled and kept walking. "The Signora Lombardo told me you wanted to speak with me."

"I do," the Israeli said. "She's told you about the plan?"

"Yes. But you have more than sufficient family in the United States. Why me?"

"Your father was head of the *Cupola*. I figured even in his present state, he'd know of some older *capos* that might still be alive and on the outside."

"You know 'Toto's' reputation?"

"Of course. Our Americans are new arrivals on the scene. The Sicilians had it down to a science before Luciano was born."

"Who pays?"

"The Vatican Bank."

"Interesting. How many would you need?"

"Two, maybe three. Your people would be in a remote location to train our army. We wouldn't want you guys to risk going to war."

"We'd be free to do things the way we want?"

"Subject only to the Supreme Leader."

"Who would he be?"

"I don't know yet."

"The Signora Lombardo said you were to be trusted."

"Even if I'm one of 'them?'"

"Signor Caen, you think we haven't investigated your background?"

"I would hope you had."

"Then you know that to us you're like a human being in the middle of the African bushveld. You're not the predator. You're not the prey. You don't meddle in our business and we aren't involved in yours. With all due respect, Mister Caen, you are irrelevant to our lives."

"I'd like to keep it that way, Signor Riina. You'll talk to your father then?"

"Si."

"*Grazie.*"

"*Prego.*"

※

"Thank you so much for that introduction, Sandy. Now we get to the local guys. Any ideas?"

"Tomaso Aiello, far and away number one. Last I'd heard, he'd moved to the Coast. Somewhere near San Francisco, Monterey I think. A lot of made men retire out there. Giuseppe Calò's eighty-five, doing life in the slam. Same with Little Vic Amuso. Leoluca Bagarella's a kid, only 74, but his ass is frying over in Italy. I'm surprised Riina didn't mention him."

"Anyone who's not doing life?"

"Yeah," Lansky's daughter chuckled mirthlessly, "the dead ones. Wait a minute. 'Big Billy' D'Elia, former head of the

## PART TWO – CHAPTER 8

Buffalino Crime Family in Pennsylvania got out a couple of years ago. He was mostly into clean stuff, money laundering, prostitution. He'd be perfect. He's seventy."

"In the prime of his life," Ezra quipped sardonically.

"Then there's Mario Gigante from the Genovese family."

"Ninety-two. A bit long in the tooth."

"Okay, Ezra. I'll give you one name who's in the same league as Tommy 'Legs' Aiello. 'Uncle Joe' Ligambi, seventy-six, retired, former acting boss of the Philadelphia crime family. He's old school, and the cops say he quietly brought stability back to the Philadelphia-South Jersey branch of the American Mafia. The New York families had only good things to say about him, and he's been able to stay out of jail. They say he's now 'semi-retired,' whatever that means. For your purposes he'd be perfect."

"Thanks again, Sandy. That's a great start. Dennis'll probably be able to pick up the ball from here."

"You think it's difficult to manage a bunch of mad dog killers, gentlemen who insist on snuffing out other gentlemen, fifty racketeers fighting for three spots as a 'made man?'"

"I can't think of anything harder than that, Sister."

She gave him a hard stare. The kind he'd originally seen that first day in the Chapel. *Nobody better fuck with me.* Then she relaxed and smiled broadly at him.

"Tommy, I'd like you to trade places with me for one week. Just one. The great unwashed public sees Santa Cecelia as one of the fanciest private schools in the world. $21,500 a year to get into *kindergarten* for God's sake, and that's *before* you buy one school uniform or one school lunch, or go on one field trip. If precious baby girl's a boarder at the high school, it's over 60K a year before books, computers, graduation gowns, you name it. And that's a 10-month year, by the way. You think I don't know they call it 'Saint Money' behind our backs? Or despite the fact that even if we claim to have the highest standards of academic excellence, that doesn't stop people from saying, 'The only sure way to get into Santa Cecelia is if the check doesn't bounce and if the donation to the endowment fund is big enough?'"

"Yeah, this place seems to be awash in money, Sister Maureen."

"Oh yes, that it does, Mister *Capo di Capi*. But every one of those parents think they own you twenty-four hours a day, and you'd damn well better keep their precious daughter safe and *virgin* and no drugs or booze or anything else like that. Have you ever raised a teenage girl, Tommy? I can guarantee you that one hundred percent of teenage girls *want* to do all that 'good' stuff and a damn high percentage of them do. Two years back, half of the eighth grade girls, *eighth graders,* bragged about how they were giving boys blow jobs."

Aiello turned from pale to purple.

"Got you there, didn't I? And when they got called on it, these sweet little ballbusters had the gall to say, 'I don't know why you're making such a big deal about it. It's not as if we were having real sex. I mean, I'd never let a boy put his thing inside me.'

"There were times when some of these same little 'virgins' came to school wearing outfits that were so skimpy they might as well have had 'For Rent' signs hangng from their pubescent nipples. And their oh-so-protective moms got all bent out of shape when we sent those girls home and made them dress in their school uniforms."

Tommy excused himself, went into Sister Maureen's outer office, and brought back two cups of coffee from a real pot, "Not one of those Keurig machines that everyone's using today."

"Your job may sound tough, Sister, but I had to keep track not only of my boys but also of the cops and the politicians. Who's on the make, who's straight, who wants to be cut in, who's secretly wired by the Feds…?"

"I'm not saying you had the easiest job in the world, Tommy. But every day, *every day,* I have to be the cop *and* I have to be the bad guy. Sister Isabel and I sleep every night in one of the girls' dorms. Sometimes the smell of marijuana or hashish can make you nauseous. Sometimes sweet little Mary is about to screw her brains out with a boy she's snuck into her room when she thought we weren't looking. Sweet little Mary's the wildest bitch in the school. What's more, she's a bitch in heat. When she's not 'cutting' her veins, she's the ringleader who's got a drawer full of cocaine. By every rule in the book, Mary should be out on her ass in a New York minute. But that's where I'm up shit's creek. On the one hand, we can't let *anything* like that hit the airwaves or the social media because if there was even the slightest whiff of a scandal at Santa Cecelia … Do I have to say more?"

Tommy Aiello hadn't even picked up his coffee cup. He sat there, transfixed.

"Oh, and did I forget to mention that Mary's daddy just kicked in a cool half million toward the new multi-purpose assembly room?"

For the next twenty minutes, Sister Maureen expounded about other aspects of her job. Teachers who were ticked off at the Lower School principal, administrators who were so loving and friendly as they preached about the importance of good manners and the love of God for all humankind, while they connived to push out the administrator just above them so they could take her place. Teachers way past their prime who challenged you not to renew their anual contracts and who hired lawyers on contingency to sue the moneyed school if you didn't renew their contracts and give them a raise in the process.

"Yep," she concluded. "Every day's just another gentle, loving, easygoing day at the most beautiful high school campus on the Pacfic Coast, and we're only in competition with four other private, they call them 'independent,' schools for the ever-shrinking dollars that are available. Welcome to another day in Paradise."

# 9

"**MISTER AIELLO**? You don't know me and we've never met, but I'd like to talk to you for a few minutes."

"Listen, Mister Whoever-you-are. I'm not in the market for anything. Not life insurance, not some new miracle medication, which I can't afford anyway. In fact, Mister ...?"

"Caen, Mister Aiello, Ezra Caen."

"Canine?"

"Caen. Like in walking cane?"

"I'm sorry, my hearing aids don't work worth a damn. I can't afford to pay for new ones. Hell, Mister Caen, to be truthful with you, I can't afford to pay *attention*, let alone buy anything."

"Mister Aiello, I'm not trying to sell you anything. You *are* Tommy 'Legs' Aiello, are you not? Eighty-two, retired *Capo di Capi* of *Il Famiglia Supremo*, eleven years at Allenwood. Have I got it right so far?"

"Christ, man, who *are* you?"

"No one of any importance. Very few people are. I'd just like to meet with you in person for a few minutes. You might just be interested. By the way, do you know a guy named Joseph Ligambi?"

Now Tommy's interest was really piqued. "Uncle Joe. The Philadelphia family?"

"Uh-huh. You still living at 745 Elm Avenue?"

"Yes. No. Wait a minute. You've got some kind of foreign accent. Are you one of those *Ay*-rabs?"

"No, but we live in the same neighborhood. I'm Israeli. A lady you might know, Sandy Lombardo, suggested I give you a call."

"Meyer Lansky's little girl?"

"Yes."

"When would you like to come over?"

"How soon can you see me?"

"Let's see … it just so happens that my calendar's a little light today. How about an hour from now?"

"Works for me."

෴

"Why me? I'm eighty-two and I can't see lugging around a pistol, let alone a submachine gun."

"Not your job, Mister Aiello. In the old days the soldiers fought the battles on the ground and the generals sat on a nearby hill. The closest they got to the action was when the smell of cordite wafted up the hill. It's the same thing today, except the general sits in an air conditioned concrete building several miles from the fighting. They say you'll always find hundreds of men that know *how* to do something, working for the man who knows *why*."

"So what am I supposed to do, Mister Caen?"

"Same thing the generals do. Use your brain and your leadership skills to decipher the big picture – from a place where you're far enough away from the woods to see beyond the nearest tree. Of course, there's not a helluva lot of woods in Syria and Iraq to begin with. Not many mountains in ISIL's areas either."

"You think I'd be useful?"

"Absolutely. Let's be honest Tommy – may I call you that?"

"Sure, why not?"

"ISIL is in the business of death. You were in the same business for many, many years. The difference between you and the Islamic Caliphate is that they think they're involved in *Jihad*, a holy war. They're full of fire and they've got all the heat and testosterone of young men everywhere. By this time in your life, you know that revenge is a dish best served cold. I imagine you've been responsible for killing hundreds in your day."

"Three hundred seventy-one," Aiello said, neither boastful nor ashamed.

"I'll bet you yourself haven't killed more than a dozen."

"Also correct. Would you like a beer … uh … Ezra?"

"Thank you, no. But if you by some chance have Pellegrino water?"

"Matter of fact, I bought a case over at Costco a couple months ago. I think I've used two bottles." Aiello rose, went to the refrigerator, and brought back a bottle and a glass. He went back and got himself a can of Budweiser.

"Tommy, you oversaw the killings. In that way you were exactly like a general. You didn't dirty your hands. I'm sure you learned that there are many ways to kill a man. Some are much more effective than others in telling other men not to mess with you."

"Like cutting off a guy's …"

"And stuffing them down the victim's throat while he's still alive. Don't look so shocked, Tommy. When you live in my neighborhood and see what I've seen, you almost become immune to it."

"If you know all this stuff and you've seen and done it all, why do you need me?"

"You didn't lose your smarts when they put you out to pasture. You've still got the savvy and, even if you don't think so, these young guys will worship the ground you walk on ten minutes after they meet you. You project that kind of aura."

"Sounds like a deal I can't refuse. I get my self-respect back, I come out clean, I don't worry about where my next meal's coming from, and I get to work with the 'good guys' for once in my life. Count me in. One last question, though."

"Shoot."

"Naww, you said I wouldn't have to do that." He grinned. Ezra was taken by the fact that even as an octogenarian Tommy "Legs" Aiello gave the hint that in his heyday he had been a very impressive man. "My question is, who's going to be the overall leader of this adventure. Surely not the President or a *real* general."

"Well …"

"You don't know that yet?"

"I know it's not going to be me and I gather you don't want it to be you. Do you have any ideas?"

"Matter of fact, I do. But you'd better be prepared to meet the last person on Earth you'd expect to take overall command of this operation."

₰₯

"You wouldn't believe me if I told you. This might sound like the craziest thing you've ever heard, but this whole crackpot operation is beyond the craziest thing I've ever heard. And stranger things have actually worked."

"Let me get this straight," the FBI director said. "You're talking about a four-foot-eleven-inch *nun*? The outgoing head of a private *girls'* school in a town of thirty-five thousand that's gonna fall off the edge of the country when the big earthquake comes? What is this, the remake of an old Sally Field TV show?"

"Yeah. She's seventy-three and can't even *hold* a shotgun let alone shoot it."

"Ezra," Dennis O'Brien joined in, "if anybody else in the world would make a recommendation like that I'd toss him in the looney bin. Hell, man, *you'd* toss him in the looney bin. You're asking us to believe that some kind of ... of a *kids'* teacher who was once a nurse back in the day and who's never been within a thousand miles of real combat ...?"

"There's more than one kind of combat, gentlemen. I believe my intuition's correct, but I'm not asking that you take my word for it. I suggest you go out to Monterey and visit her. By the way, she has no idea of why I talked with her. Tommy Aiello just took me over to the school and introduced me as an old friend. If you decide to go, I suggest you level with her from the git-go, 'cause she's got a bullshit meter that's even better than mine."

---

"You want me to undergo any of those psychological tests or aptitude tests or whatever?"

"Nothing like that. Would you mind if we asked you to meet with a few Senators? Congressmen?"

"Hardly. The better question is would *they* be afraid to meet with a few Santa Cecelia parents? Or some nice, easygoing high school girls? Would you like me to meet with them here or on the Hill?"

"Somehow I get the feeling you'll do just fine no matter where you meet them."

---

"Are you thinking what I'm thinking, Dennis?" They'd chosen to take a commercial flight back to Dulles.

"'The Little Old Lady from Pasadena.' Tiny, sweet little lady who eats nails for breakfast. Did you feel the power or was it just me?"

"No, it wasn't just you. I can guarantee you she wasn't trying to project anything like that. Since both of us are Catholics, would you think me a sinner if I said I almost feel sorry for those … whatever we're calling 'em today?"

# 10

A SLENDER young man wearing tight jeans and a black Tee-shirt with a red flag, white circle, and whimsical black eagle in the center shuffled by. "Pedro Sanchez, twenty. He's lived in a five hundred square foot one-bedroom apartment with his girlfriend Angie Morales, seventeen, for the past eight months. He's already served time twice. Two of the 'three strikes' the state allows before they put you away for good.

"Angie's brother kicks in two hundred dollars a month toward their $700 rent.

"Angie, who works as an attendant at a local Laundromat, left school in the tenth grade and makes minimum wage. She contributes her weekly pay to the pot. Pedro's unemployed. This is Phil Gomez reporting from East Salinas for KSBW Action News 8."

"They aired that clip last month," Sister Maureen said.

"I saw it," the stocky man, only an inch or two taller than the nun, replied. "Nothing really stands out about that kid, but then again you never know what's inside. I mean, look at me, Sister. Short, stocky, nothing outstanding about me. When it came to choosing up teams, I was always the kid they chose last. I was too fat to fight and too fat to run. Thank Jesus, Mary, and Joseph my parents loved me for what I was. They told me there wasn't anything I couldn't do if I put my mind to it. They taught me that if you use your head, you don't need to be the biggest or the meanest or the strongest kid on the block."

"So what's your secret, Ricardo?"

"Not much to be secretive about. I was the first child in my family ever to go to college. Hartnell for two years, then Fresno State. Got a B.S. in computer science right when it was coming into fashion. To show you how easily I could've gone the other way, my first job was at C.T.F. Soledad State Prison. Instead of being on the inside, like a lot of the kids I knew in second grade ended up, or a prison guard, and some of those guys are even worse than the inmates, I ended up in the computer department. I climbed the ladder for the next twenty years. Nothing spectacular, just a quiet, steady guy, but I didn't make any enemies. By that time I was ready to move on. You know the rest of the story."

"Quite a story it is Señor Avelino. Your parents must be extraordinarily proud."

"Yeah, that's true. Maria worked the whole time. She's now a supervisor for the State Parks and we've moved to Point Lobos. Until two years ago, we lived with my folks in Soledad, spent what money we did have on the kids' education …"

"Four children at Santa Cecelia. Even with the scholarship aid, that's sixty thousand a year."

"Don't think we don't appreciate it. Education's the only permanent way out of East Salinas. Ricardo Junior's now in his first year at Santa Clara. Rodrigo just found out he's been accepted to Cal Poly San Luis Obispo. I get the feeling that's not why you wanted to talk, Sister Maureen."

"Some coffee, Ricardo? Hot cocoa?"

"Cocoa, please."

"You know I'm leaving Santa Cecelia at the end of this year?"

"So I've heard. Seems a shame you're going into retirement so young."

"You always were a charmer, Ricardo. I can see where the two older boys got it from. I'm seventy-three. Not only can feel it every morning when I get up, but the mirror doesn't lie."

"So what're you going to do if you don't mind my asking? Travel? A new career?"

"Actually a little of both."

During the next half hour she told him much about her new endeavor. Of course, she didn't mention everything her position entailed, only that she had been selected to teach "a few dozen" Hispanics about the same age as Avelino's eldest son something having to do with the military.

"My problem is this, Ricardo. Like all young soldiers who sign up for the army, they like the excitement, the *machismo*, of being a warrior. Most of them never stop to think that the toys they're playing with will likely kill people, and it's just as likely some of them won't come back, or if they do ..."

"I understand, Sister. Killing is something a lot of them already know. I can tell you from being at Soledad for as long as I have that it can give them a tremendous high. You're telling me it's like giving an addict a fix every day while it doesn't make sense to hope that if a man gets enough of what's making him high he'll somehow go off the stuff."

"You have any ideas, Ricardo?"

"Nothing that's a guaranteed cure-all, Sister. But maybe a suggestion."

"Anything might be helpful."

"You said the people you work with, and I trust it's the Government, will pay these guys three thousand a month, tax free, plus food, clothing, and shelter. These guys aren't used to that kind of money, so a couple hundred bucks one way or the other isn't going to change their lives when they get back. I've seen thousands of them go through the system. What they need most is not money, it's self-respect, a sense that they're something more than bad-ass Spics, brown-skinned Niggers, drug dealers and mules. Does that language shock you, Sister?"

"Hardly," the newly-appointed Field Marshall replied. "At my age, what surprises me is how little *anything* surprises me anymore. Go on, Ricardo."

"What if …?" The stocky little brown-skinned man stopped and thought for moment before he continued. "What if, instead of paying them three thousand a month you paid them two thousand …and you guaranteed that every man who wanted it, whether or not they were high school graduates, would get a four-year college education and a degree. A one-way ticket out of the ghetto. And the Government guarantees them a decent job as well?"

Sister Maureen scratched her head, closed her eyes, and leaned back in her chair. "How long before *you* retire, Ricardo?"

"Maybe another eight, ten years."

"I can't promise you a thing, you understand. But what would you think if I could get you an upward transfer into the Federal

## PART TWO – CHAPTER 10

Government for a couple of years with guaranteed return to the next step up from your present position with the state? Since you'd be on 'detached duty,' you wouldn't even have to move from home, except for a few months a year's travel around the country."

"Who would I have to kill?"

"No one. You'd be a combination recruiter and salesman. You'd be giving *La Raza* and a bunch of young men who'd otherwise be flushed down the toilet of life one helluva step up."

"Maybe Angie's right. I know we're kings of the 'hood, and the little kids look up to us and want to be just like us, but where the fuck do you think we'll be when we're thirty? There'll be tougher, younger studs screwing better looking, younger girls. Have you seen some of the thirty-year-olds in Acosta Plaza?"

"Yeah," said Pedro's closest friend Alejandro Villarreal, who'd known him since they'd met in third grade. Alejandro had steered clear of the gangs, graduated from Alisal High, and was in his second year at Hartnell Community College. Despite the different paths they'd taken, their friendship had remained solid. "Remember Irene Arias? When I was twelve, I would have given everything I owned and both my balls just to touch those …" He cupped his inward directed hands and held them in front of his chest.

"When was the last time you saw her?"

"Three weeks ago. She must weigh two hundred pounds. Four kids, born a year apart. A train wreck."

"What ever happened to Augie Salas? He had his pick of every girl in the neighborhood, maybe in all Salinas. Man, he was one dude who had it all."

"Doing twenty-to-life at Pelican Bay."

"No shit? That's the hardest core prison in the state. Maybe in the whole country."

"Speaking of good-looking women, how's Angie coming along?"

"She's not showing yet, but she's only two months gone. By the time she pops the little guy out, she'll probably be on her way to looking like the rest of 'em," Pedro said, somewhat morosely. "I suppose I'll get hit with a Court order to pay her 110% of whatever I make, which is less than nothing. You know, for all her bitching, she deserves better than that. She's the one who's been supporting me."

"You ever thought about marrying her, Pedro?"

Sanchez shrugged. "At twenty? I don't think so."

"So you're gonna throw her on the shitpile of single parenthood? I always thought you were a better man than that, my friend."

"Easy for you to say," Pedro retorted angrily. "Just 'cause you haven't knocked up your señorita yet."

Alejandro put his hands in the pockets of his skinny jeans and stood up straighter. At six feet, he was two inches taller than his *compadre*. He strode toward Sanborn Road. "That might be because we've been using protection."

Pedro looked hard at his best friend, his face betraying shock. "But that's ... that's immoral."

"Says who?"

## PART TWO – CHAPTER 10

"The Church, that's who."

"Not the whole Church. Not these days. Even though the Pope hasn't made it legal, he realizes there's a real problem. Do you have any idea how many people are living on the planet, Pedro?"

"A few million, maybe?"

"How about almost seven *billion*?"

"What's the difference?"

"It takes one thousand *million* to make one *billion*, numbnuts. Didn't they teach you anything in high school?"

"Ummm ..." Pedro mumbled. "Remember, I dropped out in the second half of the ninth grade."

"Why?"

"The Norteños ..."

"Where exactly did that get you?"

Pedro Sanchez looked down, counting the cracks in the sidewalk. The two friends walked in an uncomfortable silence up Sanborn Road. Finally, Alejandro broke the silence. "You know, Pedro, back when we were in fourth grade I always thought you were the smartest kid I ever met. That's why I always wanted to be close to you, like maybe some of your smarts would rub off on me."

Pedro suddenly felt himself choking up. As close as he'd always been to Alejandro Villarreal, his pride wouldn't let him betray any weakness. After all he was king of the hill. But then a second thought assailed him. *Kind of exactly what hill? And how come the king lives in a five hundred square foot apartment in the worst part of town? And how come the king's queen and her brother had to pay the rent?* Suddenly, as though he was looking through a long tunnel, he saw his life stretching out in front of him. He couldn't see any bright light, or, for that matter, any light at all, at the end of the tunnel.

Alejandro Villarreal didn't say anything for a few moments, but somehow he intuited his friend's pain.

"Pedro, in the early 1900s the Jews came to this country with nothing but the shirts on their backs. They'd been kicked out of almost every country in Europe. They didn't have two nickels to rub together. But they somehow found a way to live ten in a room and work eighteen hours a day to send their kids to school. African-Americans, called 'Niggers' back then, had been slaves less than a hundred years before. During the Second World War, they started something called the United Negro College Fund. They were the poorest of the poor, but they started with the slogan, 'A mind is a terrible thing to waste.' Where do you think the Jews and the Blacks are today?"

"Yeah, I know that much," Sanchez replied. "But we're different."

"How? We're human beings, just like the rest of them. Just like Anglos for that matter."

"Name me one Mexican that's made it in this country."

"I'll name you two who made in this valley and went on to make themselves legends: Cesar Chavez and Dolores Huerta? Or did you forget we learned that in fifth grade? Can you even remember Cesar Chavez's most famous words?"

Sanchez thought back to fifth grade. He smiled broadly as if this were the hardest test and he'd ever taken and he knew the answer. "*Sí, se puede*" he said softly. "Yes, we can."

"You might not know it, *hermoso*, but that was Barack Obama's campaign slogan when he ran for President eight years ago. If a black man can be President, why can't one of ours?"

## PART TWO – CHAPTER 10

"Never happen," Pedro said.

"Oh, really? Try telling that to Julian or Joaquin Castro."

"You mean the Communist dictator of Cuba?"

"No, dumbshit, that's *Fidel* Castro."

"Okay. They're still Cubans, though."

"Nope. Identical twins. *Chicanos* just like us, from San Antonio, Texas, Mama was a *La Raza* activist and pretty much a single mom. Today, one of these guys is the Secretary of Housing and Urban Development for the entire United States, the other is a Congressman. Here's the biggest news of all: there's talk that either one of them might be a candidate for Vice President of the United States, one heartbeat away from the Presidency!"

"You're shitting me."

"No, my friend, I shit you not."

"Yeah, but how many Mexicans end up like that?"

"It doesn't matter if there's only one in the world. Speaking of which, Carlos Slim Helú, a Mexican, is richer than Bill Gates or Warren Buffet."

"How do you know all this shit, *muchacho*?"

"Remember what I said, 'A mind is a terrible thing to waste?' I try not to waste mine. Sure, I'm only in Hartnell, which sure as heck isn't Harvard or Stanford, but I read a lot and one day I *will* marry Sarita and we'll have kids, *two*, not half a dozen. And I'll damn sure see to it that *they* get a good education. Like Ricardo Avelino."

"Who's he?"

"You did a stretch in Soledad last year, remember?"

"How can I forget?"

"Ricardo worked there, in the computer department. He's an old guy, forty at least. Last week, he gave a talk at a Hispanic Culture lecture I attended on Saturday morning, just because I had nothing better to do. He's a short man, looks like any one of a thousand guys his age you find on just about any street in *Chicano* Salinas. He gave us this rah-rah talk about how he was the first one in his family to ever go to college, how he and wife each worked two jobs and lived with his parents and drove a fifteen-year-old Toyota Corolla to work each day for only one reason: to make sure *their* kids would have a better life than he did.

"As he kept talking, I found myself paying a lot more attention to this scruffy looking old guy than I thought I ever would. *He was selling the American Dream and he was making sense! There was no reason in the world why any of us couldn't do the same thing!* Then he started talking about his kids. All four of 'em went to school, mostly on scholarship, at Santa Cecelia, that fancy school over the hill in Monterey. The two girls went all the way through, but Saint Cecelia only goes through eighth grade for the boys. His sons finished high school at Palma, also on scholarship. Talk about a head start ..."

"That sounds wonderful," Pedro Sanchez said dejectedly, "if you've got parents like that, which happens once in maybe fifty thousand times around here. Let's face it Alejandro, I'm twenty years old, I've got an eighth grade education, two strikes against me, a pregnant girlfriend, and I don't earn shit. Maybe I once had a dream, but no more. There's nothing I can think of to get me out of this rut."

"Don't be too sure," his friend replied. "At the end of his talk, Señor Avelino mentioned something about a new program the government is working on."

# 11

The definition of "rogue state" is an amorphous one. It depends on one's point of view. If the "bad guys" do it, it's called "propaganda," but if those on "our side" do it, it's "education," or "the real truth."

There are rogue states all over the world. In the eyes of the United States of America, North Korea is a truly bad guy. Iran was a bad guy, but it's sort of on its way back to being an O.K. guy. With over seventy-nine million people it's pretty hard to ignore the 18th largest nation in the world. If you ask most Americans about tiny Israel, they'll tell you it's the only bastion of Western-style democracy in the Middle East. On the other hand, with the exception of Jordan, Egypt, maybe Turkey, and, although they'd never publicly acknowledge it, Saudi Arabia, the "little Satan" is a cancer in the world that must be eradicated at all costs.

The Turkish Republic of Northern Cyprus, TRNC for short, qualifies as a genuine rogue nation. No other country in the world except Turkey recognizes it. TRNC is not at war with anyone except the two-thirds of the swordfish-shaped 3,571 square mile island represented by the "legitimate" Republic of

Cyprus, *i.e.* the Greeks. If you believe the United Nations and the rest of the civilized world, it simply does not exist. This makes it hard to explain why a very large number of upright, law-abiding citizens from a very large number of countries who don't recognize the Turkish Republic of Northern Cyprus enjoy the beautiful Mediterranean beaches on TRNC's coast that don't exist; the ecotourism that brings millions of dollars a year to a land that doesn't exist; the luxurious hotels and casinos and the fabulous night life that don't exist; and some of the most delicious cuisine in the world which, alas, is non-existent. Like Dubai, which does exist, and Las Vegas, which certainly exists, what goes on here stays here.

Syrian National Coalition leaders meet with Baathist Assad loyalists. Jet setters who've had their fill of the Emirates or the Casino du Liban and are looking for someplace a little different nest at the Rocks Hotel Casino on the nonexistent waterfront center of TRNC's largest resort town, Kyrenia, which its Turkish inhabitants call Girne. It is not unknown for wealthy Saudi sheikhs seeking forbidden fruit to have assignations with Persian, French, English, or even luscious Balkan women at the Rocks.

Thirty-four miles to the west of Kyrenia, a group of fifteen, most of whom looked remarkably like retirees from gangster movies of thirty-five years ago or aging versions of American actor Robert De Niro, wheezed and trudged their way up twenty stairs leading to a private villa in the Troodos Mountains overlooking the Güzelyurt District and Morphou Bay. They were accompanied by a short, spry nun wearing a habit that looked more like a modest business suit that traditional sisters' garb. Incongruously, each of the men wore a thin windbreaker with the words "Poughkeepsie Teachers' College, Class of 2016," emblazoned on the back.

## PART TWO – CHAPTER 11

Once ensconced in the villa, a few marveled at the stunning scenic wonderland below them, but most headed for one of the villa's two bathrooms and stood in line, looking as uncomfortable as raw military recruits. Sister Maureen waited patiently in the capacious living room for her companions to complete their ablutions. When they returned, she confronted them as if they were mischievous, undisciplined little boys. She began without preamble.

"Gentlemen, we all know why we're here, so I won't belabor the point. If we had met somewhere in the States, it would have aroused suspicion, or at least curiosity, which is exactly what we don't need. We don't need the attention of anyone connected with our ultimate destinations. You're all veterans of wars where you never knew which of your closest associates were spying on you or had set you up. My name is Sister Maureen Richards. I was born Mary Margaret Cerone. Jackie the Lackey was my great uncle. Maybe that's why I've been detailed to head up this little project. God only knows why," she added, glancing toward the heavens as if some incalculable burden had been thrust on her shoulders.

There was genial laughter in the room, but it was tinged with a mixture of anticipation and not little bit of awe.

"First, rules," Sister Maureen began. "More particularly, consequences. If so much as one of you breaks even one of these rules, even the slightest of them, and even a little bit, you're out on your ass and in solitary in an offshore Federal penitentiary that will make Guantanamo Bay seem like Disneyland. That is if you somehow live to make it back into our hands. *Capisci?*"

Now the laughter turned nervous.

"This is our own little *Cupola*. What goes on here stays here. If anyone wants to get off the train, say so now. You'll get a free ride back home with no obligations. Anyone?"

No one raised a hand.

"Okay. On to the rules. Rule number one, this is *not* an army operation. We're not affiliated with any government, especially the United States government. We haven't been invited by any side. So far as anyone knows, we are not there. We are outlaws, plain and simple. Jungle predators, hunters, killers. Any resemblance between what an army does and what we'll be doing is purely coincidental. So the rules of warfare, the Geneva Convention, and any other code of civilized conduct does not apply to us. We're here to do a job, and that's *all* we're here to do. If any of our guys get caught, they're on their own. No embassy, no consulate, no nothing. Just like this place we're sitting in, we don't exist.

"Rule number two, we've whittled the leadership down to fifteen generals. All but one of you will be assigned to fourteen theaters, defined by geographic coordinates. Tommy 'Legs' Aiello will serve as my Chief of Staff and liaison to you fourteen sector chiefs. Each sector chief will be totally and completely in charge of his own operation. You run the entire show in your area any way you want. You are the head man, the warlord, the *Capo*. You have the complete power of life and death, with no appeal, over anyone serving under you. If they screw up or desert or turn coat, or anything except strictly obey your every word, you knock them off. Painfully, so as to make an example to others, *You* pick the weapons. Your recruits from the pool are randomly drawn.

"Rule number three, weapons. Nothing that can be remotely tied to the U.S. or to the military. No drones, no air cover, no redundancy. Most weapons will be pistols, knives, whatever comes to hand. If you have to use automatic weapons, they will look, feel, sound, and kill exactly like the firepower you used back in the day when each of you ruled your families."

"What happens if we 'liberate' weapons from the enemy?" one of the men asked.

"They become part of your arsenal. All the better because they'll confuse the Islamic State's forces and make them think they're somehow being annihilated by their own."

"What if the bad guys overrun our sector?" a pudgy graybeard inquired.

"You call Tommy or you call each general in the sectors nearest to you and, just like in the old days, they're honor-bound to come to your aid. That could, and probably will, happen from time to time."

"What's the latest estimate on how many enemy will fight?"

"Absolutely no accurate idea. We'll train twenty thousand. More if necessary. We believe their hardcore suicide fighters are somewhere around twenty thousand. There may be as many as a couple hundred thousand, but U.S. intelligence, which often seems to be an oxymoron, believes that 90% of those would cut and run if the going got tough."

"Sister, I hate to seem rude," the pudgy graybeard joined in again, "but might I ask your credentials to lead this operation?"

"Yes, you do seem rude, and my credentials are none of your goddamned business," Sister Maureen answered, but in a tone that showed she was not at all offended. "If I may ask, sir, what are *your* qualifications for being here? Got you on that one, didn't I?" she continued, smiling broadly. "Now, guys, it's time for lunch, time to pee again, and time to take a nap. There are cots for each of you, you may as well get used to the tough soldier's life. We'll assemble back here at two this afternoon and work out some details."

"So far we've got ten thousand signed up. Julian and Joaquin Castro have jumped on our bandwagon but the media has been told only that they're entering into a program to help rebuild our infrastructure. I suppose that's technically true. When we're up to twenty, we'll start the training program. The location's secret, but the generals have a need to know. For your eyes and ears only, our advanced 'schoolhouse' will be the Simpson Desert, dead in the middle of Australia. It's the world's largest sand dune desert. It has no maintained or paved roads. The Simpson Desert is so hot and dangerous, it gets up to 122 degrees Fahrenheit, that it's officially off-limits to visitors in the Australian summer, between November and February. We expect to start training our recruits next month. 'School' will last sixty days."

"How will our guys fit in? They don't speak much Spanish in *ragheadistan*." This brought a wave of sophomoric laughter.

"They'll be immersed every waking hour of every day in some dialect of Arabic. Since they won't be mixing with the local population, except to kill the most unpleasant radical segment, it's not that important that they become literate in classical Arabic poetry. But the most important part of their education will be your responsibility."

"That being the various ways to kill a man?" a squarely-built, balding patriarch asked.

"Exactly. Who better than you guys know to do that, not only most efficiently, but in such a way as to send the signal you need to send?"

"Maximum pain, maximum gain," the man responded.

"Since that'll happen mainly at night so it shakes up the daytime *jihadis* and puts them way off balance, you'll put 'em through basic training before you leave for the land Down Under, then carry on with advanced training in the desert."

For the next half hour, the retired *capi* relived their glory days of times past, each with his own rendition of how best to inflict maximum pain while, at the same time, broadcast the most meaningful message to the survivors.

As the afternoon wore on and liquor flowed, the mood lightened considerably as the sometimes-comrades, sometimes-antagonists of the past took a trip down their individual memory lanes, back to the times when the world was theirs to capture and they were filled with the fires of life, rather than the flames of arthritis.

*Part Three*

*SCHOOL DAYS
MARCH – JUNE*

# 12

JUST southeast of Bakersfield, the old blue MCI-9, a 1980s vintage former Greyhound bus, had merged onto Eastbound California Highway 58, headed for Tehachapi and Mojave. Pedro glanced at his watch. 7:45. It would be dark by eight. He'd try to get a little shuteye then. The 47-passenger bus had left Salinas four-and-a-half hours before. They'd stopped at a McDonalds somewhere in Bakersfield, then got back onto the 99.

Pedro had no idea where they were headed or even what awaited him, but whatever it was, Ricardo Avelino had told him it would be a lot better that where he'd been that morning. Since his friend Alejandro had vouched for Avelino, Pedro relaxed and looked around the bus in the fading light.

Although he thought he knew everyone there was to know in Salinas, the only familiar face on the bus was Jésus "Chuey" Garza. Pedro had known Garza very briefly and peripherally in Middle School. Chuey was a pain in the ass back then, loud, pushy, and a braggart. He'd done a stretch in Juvie when he was sixteen. When Pedro had last seen him six months ago he hadn't changed so far as Pedro could tell. It didn't disturb Pedro to see Garza. Chuey wasn't breathing his air and he was way back in the last few rows of seats. Pedro turned back to his seatmate, who seemed a nice enough dude.

"Did you finish high school?"

"Almost finished ninth grade. You?"

"Eleventh. Barely. Mister Avelino said if I made the grade there'd be college. 'No way,' I said. 'No one in our family ever made it past eleventh grade.'"

"When I told him I'd barely scraped by the ninth grade and not even the whole year, he told me there were programs," Pedro replied. "I wonder what he meant when he said '*If* we made the grade?' I thought the army took everyone."

"Yeah," his neighbor replied. "But this is not the army."

"Aren't we gonna do the same things the army guys do? Kill the bad guys?"

"That's what I thought. But Mister Avelino said this was not the army. We wouldn't be in the military and the government wouldn't even admit we existed. There are a lot of holes in this story we don't know about."

"So why are you here, Miguel? And by the way, my name is Pedro Sanchez."

"Miguel Hernandez," he said, shaking Pedro's hand. "Why are *you* here?"

They glanced meaningfully at one another, a look that answered both their questions. *Exactly what the fuck else presents a better alternative?*

"You got any idea where we're headed?" Pedro asked.

"Nope. Some guy mentioned Homey Airport. Someone else in the line said Groom Lake. Never heard of either of them."

## PART THREE – CHAPTER 12

Pedro Sanchez pushed the recliner button and the seatback reclined. Very little.

He did not know how much time had gone by when he was awakened by a noisy scuffling in the back. He kept his eyes closed, trying to ignore it, but it got louder and he heard coarse swearing. Half-opening one eye, he looked back, then, shocked into wakefulness, he looked harder and saw two guys going at one another with knives. One of them was Chuey Garza.

The driver said something into a cell phone, slowed down, and pulled off the road. He levered the front door open. Two older guys, very large, who looked like they would take no shit from anyone, entered the bus. Without so much as a glance or a word, the two gorillas elbowed their way toward the rear.

The two combatants, oblivious the approaching giants, kept slashing at each other. Suddenly, one of the older men seized Garza by the throat, while his companion did the same to Chuey's antagonist. Seconds later, the fighters' faces had gone purple. Choking, they dropped their knives and started to slump to the floor. They never made it that far. Each was grabbed by his tight jeans and dragged to the front door of the bus, where the larger of the behemoths gave each of the Hispanics a push-kick that sent them reeling to the asphalt shoulder six feet below.

One of the large men stepped off the bus and singlehandedly hauled the moaning Chicanos into the brush adjacent to the road. The other man stood and addressed the rest of the passengers.

"Okay, assholes. You've just seen what happens when someone doesn't listen to the lecture they gave you back in Salinas. You guys are going to be a *team*. You're damn well going to act like a team, or you're going to be fucked, understand?"

In the shock of the moment, no one said anything. Finally, one of the passengers meekly asked, "Sir, what's going to happen to those two guys?"

"They're not going to be killed and they're not going to be roughed up ... very much. They're simply going to wake up with a helluva headache and some pretty good bruises. And they'll have a lovely little walk back to Salinas."

With that, he exited the conveyance. The bus pulled out. They were on the highway again. Pedro Sanchez fell asleep within minutes.

When the forty-five remaining passengers arrived at their destination via what the signs called the Extraterrestrial Highway at 9:00 a.m. on March 13, it was a balmy seventy-eight degrees. Pedro counted twenty-three similar buses parked in a large gravel parking lot adjacent to four gigantic gunmetal gray hangars marked "4," "5," "6" and "7."

"Must be over a thousand guys here," he remarked to Miguel. "Every one of them looks like *la Raza,* and from what I can see, all of 'em are our age."

Just then four jet aircraft roared by at low altitude, their wake leaving the loudest sound Pedro Sanchez had ever heard. Although he involuntarily clamped both hands over his ears, he could not escape the violent tremors that shook the ground under his feet. His eyes were drawn to the advanced fighter craft, which suddenly turned and soared straight up, not seeming to lose any speed. Within seconds, when they were almost out of sight, they entered into a steep dive and turned southeast toward the direction from which they'd originally come.

When Pedro Sanchez turned to look at the others standing in the parking lot, he saw that, like him, their faces were uniformly awestruck by what they'd just seen. Moments later, the desert surrounding them was silent, except for the movement of a thousand young Mexicans being herded toward one of the hangars.

Within minutes, Pedro found himself in the fourth hangar, which had been set up in divided barracks, four rows of twenty-five upper-and-lower bunk beds with small cabinets at the head and on each side of the beds. Each of the barracks slept two hundred men. The hangar contained six barracks, along with latrines, showers, and washrooms sufficient for the inhabitants. The air conditioners were turned on full blast.

A nondescript, squarely built man about thirty-five stood at the entrance to the hangar. Every two minutes, he would call out sharply, "Find a bunk. Put whatever you brought with you on the bunk. Take the numbered tag off your bunk and carry it with you. The same number is on your headboard, so you won't get confused when you come back. Don't worry, no one will steal your stuff. Line up at the other side of the hangar. Someone there will send you to the quartermaster for clothing and supplies. It's now oh-nine-forty. When you get your stuff, bring it back and hang it in the closet next to your bunk. Carry your numbered tag with you at all times. Meet back here at eleven-forty. That'll give you two hours before mess."

His orders were quick, direct, no nonsense, and brooked no questions.

Pedro Sanchez and Miguel Hernandez, who'd become fast friends during the journey from Salinas, decided to room together.

"Up or down?" Pedro asked.

"Doesn't matter to me. Wanna' flip a coin for it?"

"Yeah, why not a peso?"

"Suits me."

They flipped. Pedro drew the upper bunk.

"I hope you don't wet your bed, amigo," Miguel said lightly. "I don't sleep too well with piss dropping on my head."

"Don't worry, *muchacho*. Last I could tell, I was housebroken."

They picked up their yellow tags, marked to indicate the barracks number. 178-A for Hernandez, 178-B for Pedro Sanchez. An hour-and-a-half later each returned to his "bedroom" with two pair of khaki shirts and slacks, two pairs of gym shorts, a baseball cap, a sweatshirt, a Tee-shirt, three pair of underwear, thick socks, a pair of running shoes, and hard-toed black shoes, Brogans, all of which fit surprisingly well. At 11:30, ten minutes before they'd been told to return to the front of the hangar, they presented themselves to the same broad-shouldered man who'd greeted them less than two hours before.

"I'm not familiar with military talk," Miguel told Pedro. "But I think 'mess' means food. It sounds like slop to me."

Hernandez was wrong. The 'slop' turned out to be a chow line, a buffet featuring some of the best food he'd ever eaten. There was as much as he wanted to eat and more.

A raised stage stood at one end of the mess hall. When most of the fellows had eaten their fill and were drinking carbonated soft drinks and belching to get rid of excess gas, a group of people gathered on the raised stage: eight old men, all dressed alike, tight suits and ties. Had Pedro Sanchez ever seen an old gangster movie, which he had not, or read a newspaper or newsmagazine from the 1980s or before, which he also had not, the look of these "suits" would have been obvious and instantly recognizable. High-risen gangsters of the type that ate Norteños for lunch and spit out the bones.

What was even more incongruous, a tiny woman in blue nun's habit approached the lectern and walked directly to the middle of the stage. Pedro, who'd been raised a Roman Catholic, certainly recognized a nun when he saw one,

The guys kept on eating and talking spiritedly, hardly paying attention to the gathering on the stage. As invariably happens, in a large room full of noisy, active people, it is the one person who stands silently, saying nothing, who eventually captures the attention of everyone in the room. So it happened here. The noise and bustle slowly died down, like air leaking out of a balloon. It wasn't long before all eyes centered on the small nun.

When everyone was silent, the woman said, "Please join me in the Lord's Prayer." Over a thousand young men's voices obeyed, over a thousand young men stood, driven by a powerful force, praying in unison. When they finished, the woman said, "You may be seated." Then, "Gentlemen, I would like to introduce you to some very important people. You will see them today. Thereafter, it will be some time before you see them again."

The eight old men, ranging from five-feet one inch in height to over six feet tall stood and came forward. Each looked like someone you would not care to meet in a dark alley at night. Each sported a bulge in the breast pocket of his tight-fitting jacket which did not appear to be a cell phone or a brassiere.

The nun introduced them, starting with the smallest and moving up. "General Gigante." There was nervous titter as the absurdly-named little man, who looked as old as a Biblical patriarch, stepped forward. A glare from him stopped the laughter in its tracks.

"General Riina from the island of Sicily."

"General Lucchese." At five-foot seven, he seemed to be the youngest of the group, just over seventy.

She continued. "Any one of you ever been to Philadelphia?" No one raised a hand. "If you'd have been there a few years ago, you would undoubtedly have heard of the next man, General Ligambi." A couple men started to applaud, then stopped in mid-clap.

She picked up the pace slightly as she introduced the next three. "General DiCavalcante; General Dragna from L.A.; General Aiuppa." The seven men returned to their seats, leaving the tallest man standing.

"Finally, gentlemen, my Chief of Staff, Generalissimo Aiello." Tommy "Legs" nodded slightly. He gave off a sense of faded, though genuine, dignity. "Thank you, Sister," he said politely, taking the microphone from her. "Boys, this lady is Sister Maureen Cerone Richards. I am sure you are all wondering what she is doing here. The answer is simple. Sister Maureen is the boss man of the entire program, the Field Marshal.

"I want to make one thing very clear: you show her disrespect even once, even for the smallest infraction, you are out on your ass with no warning. The nearest town's Las Vegas, a long way down the road, and you'll have a nice walk, provided you make it. You disobey *anything* she asks you to do a second time, you don't walk out of here. They will find your dead ass ground up and buried beneath three tons of concrete or three tons of desert. If you think I'm kidding, I suggest that any you who're computer literate and have access to Google look up a guy named Jimmy Hoffa. Gentlemen, you're now going to go back to your barracks and take a nap. For the next three weeks you're gonna work harder than you've ever worked in your lives. By the time you leave this place, you're going to be superman-clones, men of steel. So I suggest you get all the rest you can. Gentlemen, at-*ten-SHUT!*" They jumped up as one. "Dis-MISSED!"

༺༻

"Holt shit, Miguel, what the *fuck* did we sign up for?" Pedro spoke softly to his bunkmate on the way back to their beds.

"Don't know," the other replied. "But 'men of steel' sounds exciting to me."

༺༻

Exciting it might have sounded, but the old saw "No pain, no gain" was more than accurate. The next morning, reveille sounded at 4:30 a.m. Ten huge drill instructors (God knows what army they came from, but undoubtedly it was the army from hell!) waited at the front door of the hangar as the half-asleep recruits relieved themselves, pulled on their shorts, sweatshirts, and running shoes which the quartermaster had doled out to them, and groggily stumbled out the front door.

"Okay, pussies, time to start shapin' up!" a fierce looking black man shouted. "We let you guys sleep an hour more than you needed. In that hour you must've put on two pounds of ugly fat. Get your asses out onto yonder field and we'll do some warmup exercises before we start our little trot!"

Thirty minutes later, after a series of jumping jacks, sit-ups, burpees, running in place, and pushups, the soon-to-be man of steel, Pedro, noted it was ten of six. He stood up, panting. A slimmer *anglo* took over from the black man.

"Ladies, it's time for a relaxing little jaunt before we have a bite to eat, if that's all right with you. Even if it isn't, we're going to have a little trotty-poo anyway. Follow me!"

What followed, the little "trotty-poo," turned out to be a three-mile run through the desert, which, Pedro soon discovered, was anything but flat. Up sand dunes, down steep rock-strewn pathways, around sharp bends. Even though Sanchez considered himself to be in reasonably good shape, by a mile-and-a-half he was sweating profusely and his throat felt parched and sore because of his heavy panting.

"C'mon Sanchez, get your lazy ass in gear!" shouted Miguel, who'd been running ahead, but who'd taken the time to circle back to goad his friend on. "You ain't fifty yet, and you're chuggin' along like an old man!"

Pedro swore good-naturedly, stopped, took a few deep breaths, and started running again. Fortunately, the last part of the run back to the base was mostly mild downhill on hard-packed earth. Sanchez noted that the running coach was neither sweating nor breathing hard when he got back to the field. Pedro realized, not without pride, that he and Miguel were in the front third of all the runners.

"Okay, guys," a third trainer said. "For a bunch of sixty-year-olds, you didn't do too badly. Wonder how you might have done had you been racing the generals you met yesterday. Chow's ready in the mess hall, then it's morning class."

Breakfast was every bit as hearty and delicious as lunch and dinner had been the day before. Afterward, the trainees were directed to another huge hangar, this one made up of several classrooms, theaters, workout rooms, and gyms.

A pleasant, recorded female voice came over the Public Address system as they entered the huge building. "Take any empty seat you find in any theater. Every seat's as good as any other. You'll be able to see and hear well from anywhere in the room. You need not take notes. There will not be any tests after this session. Class lasts two hours. If you have to go to the latrine I suggest you do so now. Class starts in fifteen minutes."

As Miguel, Pedro, and two hundred others entered the first theater on the left, they found themselves in a large room with a full-sized movie screen. When everyone was seated, a male speaker, a foreigner by his clothing and accent, appeared on the screen. "Good morning, recruits," he said. "My name is Mohsin al Jaballah. As you might surmise, I am not a native-born American. I am thirty-one years old. I was born and grew up in Mosul, two-hundred-fifty miles north of Iraq's capital, Baghdad. When I left my homeland at the end of 2013 to teach Islamic Religious Studies at Princeton University, 2½ million people lived in Mosul. In early 2014, *ad-Dawlah al-Islāmiyah fī 'l- 'Irāq wa-sh-Shām,* Daesh, the Islamic State, came to town. Since that time, half a million people have left Mosul.

"The motion picture you are about to see tells the story about the Islamic Caliphate. Many of you will find it shocking and disgusting. Some of you will find yourself becoming nauseous and may need to excuse yourself to go to the restroom and vomit. That is acceptable. The purpose of these and similar lessons will be to show you exactly what you'll be up against and why it's so very important that you learn to build up resistance to the sickening sights you will see. While many of you are used to some degree of violence and even murder in your own backyard, you will never have experienced it on this scale. To survive this pernicious disease on the fringes of humanity, you must not only bite off its head, but you must bury its tail deep within the desert so that it may not emerge to feed on civilized people. Gentlemen, I thank you for your time. Let us move on to the motion picture." The lights went all the way down.

A muezzin's call to prayer. A close-up of a minaret. As the camera pulled away for a long shot, the never-ending desert hove into view. An empty land of bone-dry undulating hills and valleys. A place to be *from*.

The audience viewed a series of almost stereotypical scenes: crowded *souks,* Middle Eastern markets; men bowing toward the east as they worshiped Allah five times a day, a mule pulling a cart laden with textiles along a city street half-filled with ten-year-old Toyotas, Opels, even the occasional Mercedes. Modern towns rising from naked desert. In the midst of this, a car driven into the center of a large public square. A bomb blast which decimated the area and left shrieking, wailing women, their heads covered in conservative Islamic hoods. A close up of the destroyed vehicle with a black *Jihad* standard painted on the side.

The camera moved to a desert outpost which could be anywhere in the Middle East. Men in black, their heads and bodies covered, the only visible signs of their human appearance being the slits in their eyes. An uncovered man standing between them, hopelessness in his eyes as the covered men unceremoniously chopped off both hands, just above the wrists. Cut to another scene; a similar group hacking off a man's head at the neck. Close-up of a black *jihadi* flag followed by a voice over.

"The Islamic State of Iraq and Syria, sometimes called ISIS, sometimes called ISIL, the Islamic State of Iraq and the Levant, a Salafi jihadist militant group that follows an Islamic fundamentalist Wahhabi doctrine of Sunni Islam. The group is also known as Daesh, an acronym derived from its Arabic name. It claims religious, political and military authority over all Muslims worldwide."

The camera showed a similarly black-garbed group of men beating and stoning several women as they ran screaming into the desert.

"The group's ideas of a caliphate have been widely criticized. The United Nations and mainstream Muslim groups reject its statehood. As of December 2015, the group had control over vast landlocked territory in Iraq and Syria, with a population estimated at between three and eight million people, where it enforces its interpretation of Sharia Law. ISIS affiliates control small areas of Libya, Nigeria and Afghanistan, and operate in other parts of the world, including North Africa and South Asia."

Cut to a map showing arrows and a black stain expanding over areas controlled by the Islamic State.

"In early 2014, ISIS drove Iraqi government forces out of key cities in its Western Iraq offensive, followed by the capture of Mosul and the Sinjar massacre. The possibility of a collapse of the Iraqi state prompted a renewal of United States military action in the country. In Syria, the caliphate has conducted ground attacks on both government forces and rebel factions. The Islamic State claims it has 40,000 fighters, with the majority being Iraqi and Syrian nationals."

Filmclips of horrendous and graphic torture, killings, mayhem. The bombings in Brussels and Paris.

"Adept at social media, ISIS became notorious for its videos of beheadings of soldiers and civilians, journalists and aid workers, and for the destruction of cultural heritage sites, such as in Tadmur in Syria. The United Nations holds ISIS responsible for human rights abuses and war crimes. Amnesty International has charged the group with ethnic cleansing on an historic scale in Northern Iraq. Islamic religious leaders around the world have overwhelmingly condemned ISIS's ideology and actions, arguing that the group has strayed from the path of true Islam and that its actions do not reflect the religion's real teachings or virtues."

A roll of nations and organizations scrolling up the screen.

"The group has been designated a terrorist organization by the United Nations, the European Union and its member states, the United States, India, Indonesia, Israel, Turkey, Saudi Arabia, Syria, Iran ... Over 60 countries are directly or indirectly waging war against the Islamic State."

For the next ninety minutes scene followed grisly scene. Gore, blood, intestines spilling onto the ground, drownings, explosions, humiliations followed by more killings. Cutting off of water. Incredibly beautiful, meaningful ancient temples and monuments obliterated, blown up, destroyed.

"Confusion, terror, fear undulating through the countries, a firestorm of unparalleled destruction. Whom do we support? A government so demoralized it doesn't know where to move next? A bloodthirsty son of a bloodthirsty dictator, who, at least, seems able to keep parts of his country stable? A thousand different rebel armies, each with its own agenda? Utter chaos? *Is there an answer anywhere?*"

"ربك أ لله" flashes on the screen.

"*Allahu Akbar. <u>Takbir</u>.* God is the greatest! But who commands the right to say *whose* God is the greatest? The

Kurds? The Turks? The Sunnis? The Shi'ites? The Alevi? The Islamic State? The 'civilized' Western world?

"The Caliphate accepts no boundaries. Europe trembles, waiting for the next dreadful, completely unexpected deluge of death. Will it be in Charlie Hebdo's headquarters in Paris? Zaventem International Airport in Brussels? San Bernardino, California? Can you trust anyone with darker skin? Anyone who speaks with an accent and won't look you in the eye? Must we destroy every single follower of Islam everywhere in the world? Do we risk becoming an extension of the terror that sickens us?"

Cut to a black-and-white picture of thousand of Nazis goose-stepping at a rally in Nuremberg in 1935. Cut to a color shot of Serbs and Bosnians stabbing, shooting, killing, bombing each other in Sarajevo. Music of the 1962 Bob Dylan song as the motion picture slowly fades out.

> "How many roads must a man walk down
> Before you call him a man?
> How many seas must a white dove sail
> Before she sleeps in the sand?
> How many times must the cannon balls fly
> Before they're forever banned?
>
> The answer, my friend, is blowin' in the wind
> The answer is blowin' in the wind.
>
> How many years can a mountain exist
> Before it is washed to the sea?
> How many years can some people exist
> Before they're allowed to be free?
> How many times can a man turn his head
> And pretend that he just doesn't see?

The answer, my friend, is blowin' in the wind
The answer is blowin' in the wind.

How many times must a man look up
Before he can see the sky?
How many ears must one man have
Before he can hear people cry?
How many deaths will it take 'til he knows
That too many people have died?

The answer, my friend, is blowin' in the wind
The answer is blowin' in the wind.

The screen darkened for a moment. Then the following words appeared in white letters:

"CHANGE DOES NOT COME WHEN ONE SEES THE LIGHT
CHANGE COMES WHEN ONE
NO LONGER WANTS TO LIVE IN THE DARKNESS."

The house lights slowly came up.

# 13

"**Christ,** what a fucked-up shithole of a town this is," Chuey Garza remarked morosely to the young Latino walking next to him. "I am so sorry I got involved in that fight with you, Jorge."

"Yeah, that goes double for me, *hermoso*. How did we even get started?"

"Don't know, don't remember. Some guy shoved me and I thought it was going to be a rumble. Since I'd come prepared I made sure *my* blood wasn't gonna be spilled."

After they'd been thrown off the bus and roughed up, they'd quickly forgotten that moments before they were trying to kill each other. They checked as best they could in the dark to see that no bones were broken and that everything seemed to be in the place it was supposed to be. It was going to be a long night, but thankfully it had not been particularly cold. By curling up in an area of brush some twenty feet off the highway, they'd managed to sleep until sun-up, five forty-five according to Garza's watch. By that time, their bodies ached from the pummeling and each had a black eye. No fun.

After relieving themselves in the brush, they tried to decide the best course to take. It would be a long walk either way, but Jorge Robles had the presence of mind to remember they were headed east toward Tehachapi and they hadn't yet come to that town when they'd been discharged from the bus carrying the other guys. He knew they'd left Bakersfield about an hour before. That'd be sixty miles walking back to Kern County's metropolis. At the rate of two or three miles an hour, it would take them two or three days to get back there unless they could somehow thumb a ride. They turned east. By 9:00 a.m. they reached their destination.

Tehachapi, California, population one jackass, four pine cones, and an apple. A big women's prison with lots of guard towers. The usual fast food places. Cheap, but it wasn't great when you didn't have two dimes to rub together.

Neither Jorge Robles nor Jesus "Chuey" Garza was above panhandling, but there wasn't a Chicano face to be found. The music blaring from a 1990s vintage Cadillac was distinctly Bakersfield country and western. Welcome to hell.

As the day went by, the two men became hungrier and hungrier. They cadged some coffee at McDonalds by waiting until two customers had left the remainder of their meal on the table rather than walking three feet to the nearest waste bin and shoveling the paper cups into the basket. They seized the two cups and went to the counter. "Could we get a refill, please?" Jorge asked the attendant, one of the very few Mexican faces he'd seen all day.

"Sure," the young Latina replied. She reached back for the coffee pot and filled each of their cups. "You guys look pretty hungry," she said. "If you don't mind me saying so, you look like you've been dragged through a wringer pretty badly."

## PART THREE – CHAPTER 13

"That's for sure, *mamacita*," Chuey remarked. "Our car got a flat tire about fifteen miles west of here. When we pulled over, a coupla' black dudes jumped us, beat the shit out of us, and took all our money and identification. We waited in the car until it got light, then figured no one was going to pick us up, so we started walking."

"I'm so sorry. I wish I could give you guys something to eat, but the assistant manager's an asshole and I'd lose my job if I even tried to give you anything. Have you tried the police station?"

"Don't know where it is. Don't know what it's like," Jorge chimed in.

"For a *Raza*, not good at all," she said. "We seem to be of the wrong persuasion as far as the rednecks are concerned."

"Man, we are some hungry *cholos*," Jorge continued. "Is there any place we could even hole up for tonight? Maybe get *something* inside so we could look for day jobs tomorrow?"

"There is one place I can think of," she said. "They say they take anyone in. They've got a sign over the door, 'Give me your tired, your poor.'"

"Hey, sister, any port in a storm."

"It's a little mosque on the wrong side of the tracks. Not much more than a shack, but you might find something to eat and a place to bed down."

⁂

"Of course you are welcome, my brothers," the man said gently. He looked young, perhaps four or five years older than they were. His skin color was remarkably close to theirs, his clothing was simple, and he seemed to understand their plight perfectly.

"I'm so sorry this happened to you. Victims of racial warfare, but you can't seek out the law enforcement agencies because you are of the wrong race. Of course, it makes their lives easier if they let the underclass kill off one another. To them you're just jigaboos or spics. Allah forbid they should see you as ordinary human beings."

"You got that right Mister …"

"Jarallah. Ahmed Al-Jarallah."

"You say this place is a house of worship?"

"That it is. Doesn't look like much, does it?" the smaller man smiled ruefully.

"Well …" Chuey said ambiguously.

"You are very diplomatic," Jarallah responded. "Of course, it is not the size or richness of the house of worship that counts," he continued. "The size of the spirit is the size of the pure heart. A carpet can be a temple if one prays from it sincerely."

"I never met a Muslim," Jorge said. "What you say makes a lot of sense."

"Then your receptive heart is greater than the strength of your assailants …"

"The guys that jumped us," Garza said.

"That is so. Please have some more lamb stew and sweet mint tea," Jarallah said.

He spooned some more of the rich mixture onto their plates and poured the aromatic beverage from an urn. "How old are you fellows? Twenty-one? Twenty-two?"

## PART THREE – CHAPTER 13

"About that," Garza said, pleased that the cleric had recognized they were not children but mature men.

"I gather there are times you feel uncomfortable in your society. Wrongfully shunned? People who don't understand you …?"

"You've got that right, Mister Jarallah."

"You may call me *Imam* if you prefer. In our culture that means a teacher or a priest. Someone whose job in life is to serve others, not to lord it over them. I feel humbled to be in your presence Señor Garza, Señor Robles."

"Imam Jarallah, you seem wise in the ways of the world, yet so understanding," Jorge ventured. "Surely there's some purpose we could serve larger than ourselves," he continued.

"I trust you've never traveled outside your country?"

"Mister Imam Jarallah, Chuey and I have never traveled outside Central California."

"So much to be done …" Jarallah murmured.

"What do you mean?" Garza asked.

"I come from a country called Syria. I'm a Salafi Sunni Muslim. We are a proud people. We celebrate the value of each human being, no matter what his religion. If one lives by the precepts of the Quran, *Sharia,* you come to realize you are an integral part of a greater whole. My people desire to bring peace and *wholeness* to the world through *Sharia*, but there are forces of ultimate evil who now rule my country, who deny religious freedom, who spit on what you Americans call democracy. You've no doubt heard of Bashar al-Assad?"

"I think so," Garza said. "Isn't he some kind of dictator that America was trying to get rid of?"

"Ah, you are not only intelligent and perceptive, but you keep your antennae tuned to worldwide news events."

Chuey preened, both at the cleric's acknowledgment of his intelligence and at this man's appreciation of his sophistication.

"As I'm certain you are aware Señores, fortunately for my country there are forces bonding together to bring true freedom to our land, to fight, and hopefully to unseat, the dictator. But we are in need of humanitarian aid to feed our hungry, clothe our naked, protect our women and children. We cannot do this alone. It is so easy for the forces of the dictator to recognize us and ferret us out, even if we are only a small minority. We desperately need volunteers to help us in our worthy cause. Our forces have created the only viable alternative to dictatorship, a true Islamic State. So far, we have made inroads in Iraq and Syria. With Allah's help, we will one day bring light to the world."

"But *Imam* Jarallah," Robles asked. "Aren't there those who don't want to see the light?"

"Perhaps, my brothers," the imam remarked. "But it is said among my people, 'Change does not come when one sees the light. Change comes when one no longer wants to live in the dark.'"

Both young Latinos very much warmed to this small man and his very large message.

"Assuming, Imam Jarallah, that we wanted to join in this fight, bring humanitarian aid to your land, how would we go about doing it? We have no money here or now. Even back in Salinas we had very little money and no opportunity."

"If the heart longs to go, the heart will find a way," the imam replied gently. "We have some funds, not much but enough. My people will somehow arrange to fly you to Chicago and from there to Istanbul. When you get to Turkey, our friends will help you get to the Syrian frontier and then over the border into my country. From there, Allah will guide your footsteps in the path of right and righteousness. Nor need you be alone. We have very lovely young women in our homeland that I can assure you will be entranced by your presence. There is no need to forego the delights they offer simply because you are fighting in Allah's army…. Meanwhile, what better way to finish off the evening than some of the best baklava you'll ever taste? And, of course, some more mint tea."

# 14

By the end of the second week, Pedro had not only accommodated to the training schedule, but he found he actually enjoyed it. Up at 4:30, exercises, the run, which had now lengthened to five miles, a mammoth breakfast, followed by morning class. His days at high school had been boring. He'd felt like the class dummy. Not here. For the first time in his life, Pedro Sanchez learned the incredible magic of feeling, *I can understand it. I can do it, and I never thought I could!*

History, geography, culture, religion, all these things tied in together and made *sense* to him. He began to question the *why* of things. Even when he napped at 1:30 in the afternoon, even when he lay down exhausted at 8:00 at night, it was as though the machine in his head didn't stop running.

He found himself using his newfound knowledge to grapple with *physical* matters as well. After a light afternoon sleep, when he went to *krav maga* or some other discipline for hand-to-hand combat, he found himself asking, "*Why* does such-and-such a movement work so much better than simply lashing out with fists? Why am I able to do so much better when I *think ahead* to what I should do next: plan it out instead of explode in anger?

Without noticing it, Pedro Sanchez felt so much more energized. He ate better than he had at any time during his life. He made it a point to do *more* than what was required. For the first time ever, he looked forward to the coming day with anticipation that it was going to be better than the last.

It all came home to him at the beginning of the second week, when Miguel commented, "Man, you are really starting to look and act like a man of steel." That elation was underscored when, the following day, his teammates – the instructors had arbitrarily broken the men up into groups of ten – unanimously elected him their team leader.

The most intriguing part of school happened on Wednesday, Thursday, and Friday afternoon of the second week. When he arrived at his martial arts class at three o'clock on Wednesday, the usual instructors were not there. Instead, there were two strangers, a slender middle-aged man with a pencil moustache, and an obese, slightly older man who looked like he could kill you by *sitting* on you.

"Gentlemen," their barracks head said. "Up 'til now you've learned about eastern hand-to-hand fighting, the so-called 'gentle way.' Special Forces in the U.S. Army learn that kind of stuff. It's clean, it's gentlemanly, and it's a good way to defend yourself and put off an attacker. That's all very nice, very sportsmanlike, very traditional. It is most definitely *not* the way we're going to operate when we get to our ultimate destination.

He turned to the man on his right and the larger man on his left.

"You're about to start learning what's *different* about the way *we're* going to war. We're not going to teach these savages how to be nicer, we're going to teach them that you don't fuck with *our* army. If they mess with us, they're going to get a lesson in *pain management*. They're going to have to manage the pain they suffer until they'll be eager to die, and the word will go out to their *compadres*."

Moments later, he introduced the smaller of the two men, Artie "Dandy" diGirolamo , and the huge man, Max "Fats" Bruno.

DiGirolamo invited the class to sit on chairs spread around the room. He wheeled out a plastic skeleton and a power-point screen of the type of chart one would see in a doctor's office.

"The first thing we're gonna learn is what parts of the human body are the most sensitive to pain, where you'll get the biggest bang for the buck. I'm sure each of you guys knows the seat of all pain, which is place where you get the most pleasure. Yes, you in the chair to the left?" he said, pointing to a mid-sized Hispanic.

"The *cojones*?"

"Absolutely. The balls, the family jewels, the testicles. You've heard the saying, 'When you've got 'em by the short hairs their hearts and minds will follow.' That's not just based on real pain, it's based on *perceived* pain, you know what I mean?"

"Yes sir." Pedro Sanchez was surprised to find himself responding. "That's the very heart of man. Not only what he needs to screw, but what he needs to make babies who'll carry his seed forward. What he needs that will make him, in his own mind, bigger, stronger, and more *virile* than other men."

"Holy shit, Sanchez, where'd you get that kind of smarts?" Miguel asked. Pedro noticed his friend was awed by that answer.

"That's absolutely correct, Mister …?"

"Pedro. Pedro Sanchez, sir."

"Good thinking, Mister Sanchez. Let's see if I can trip a smart fellow like you up. It's the source of what a man sees as his strength, but what else?"

"Despite a man talking about 'having a hard-on,' the balls and the sack holding them are the softest part on a man's body, meaning he wants to protect them before any other part."

"Well said, Mister Sanchez," DiGirolamo said. "By the way, a woman's most sensitive parts are in the same area. That surprised some of you, didn't it? Better learn you'll be coming across almost as many female soldiers as males. They used to refer to it as a 'honey trap' back in the day. Would any of you feel the slightest hesitation to whack a woman's pussy with the stock of your rifle? I see some of you looking pretty squeamish. Better get used to it, guys. If it comes down to her snatch or your gonads you're gonna have to make that decision in a split second."

One of the men got up shakily and stumbled out of the room.

"That's okay," DiGirolamo continued. "Better he gets sick now and toughens up later. You're all going to be faced with that decision sooner or later and you better get used to it. Contrary to what President Bush said, we do *not* know how these people think. They do *not* think like us. So *we're* the ones that have to be smarter, quicker, more creative in how we inflict pain. That means we fight in *their* sandbox *our* way, which is the only way to keep 'em off balance. Let's take a little break for some bread and water."

The little break took less than five minutes. The trainees now sat nervously on the edge of their seats, their eyes and ears riveted on the little man with the moustache.

"Let's look at some other major pain points."

DiGirolamo explored in detail where you could hurt a man most: the inside of the elbows, the kneecaps, the ankles, the fingers, the wrists, the nose, eyes, ears, cheekbones, the bottom of the feet …

"The Turks taught us that last one," he said. "Tie a man down so he's lying on his back and his feet are bare. Take a hard object, any type of club, a baseball bat, whatever. Hit him on the bottom of his feet steadily, over and over and over again. It doesn't even have to be that hard. Within an hour, two at most, the guy won't have a mark on his body but his own mother wouldn't recognize him. He'll sure as hell be so crazy with pain and terror he wouldn't recognize his own mother. Nice touch. The Turkish cops still use it today. Very effective."

"Anywhere else, sir?" This from the back of the room.

"I think I've covered most of standard ones. But you can always improvise. I'm a little guy. In my game, you always come up against bigger, stronger guys. You don't always have time to figure what you're gonna do with Tae Kwon Do, Jiu Jitsu, or that kind of stuff."

"Mister DiGirolamo, what's the most original way you ever killed a man?"

"Another good question Mister Sanchez. I'm gonna keep an eye on you to make sure my own back's safe."

There was a rush of laughter from the recruits, the kind of laughter that comes when it's necessary to relieve what could become unbearable stress.

"Come on up here, Mister Sanchez. I'll demonstrate in very slow motion. I promise I won't hurt you."

Sanchez was half a foot taller than DiGirolamo.

DiGirolamo drew back his right arm, extended his right hand with fingers straight and tight together, took calculating aim, and drove his hand very slowly like a spear into Pedro's solar plexus, stopping just short of Sanchez's belly. Imagining what it would feel like if "Dandy" had moved in anything but slow motion, Pedro involuntarily clutched at the pit of his stomach.

DiGirolamo reared his rigid right hand back, then drove it, again very slowly and stopping short of the mark, into Pedro's Adam's apple. Finally, DiGirolamo, using his stiffened hand like the flat blade of a knife, swung it sideways at the underside of Sanchez's nose, stopping just before he hit paydirt. The smaller man was not even breathing hard, nor had he worked up any kind of sweat.

"Mister Sanchez, you would now be dead," he said.

"Explain, please," Pedro demanded.

"It's all in using a stiff hand. You can kill a man by jamming it up under his breastbone and tearing his guts, or you can smash his Adam's apple so he strangles. Or you can hit him hard under the nose. That breaks the bone at the bridge of his nose and drives the splinters up into his brain."

He picked up a glass of water from a nearby lectern. "Okay Fats, your turn."

The larger man addressed the students.

"Guys, I'm sixty-eight years old. As you can see, I'm too fat to run and I'm too fat to fight any of you without a little help from my friends."

He extracted a small handgun from his breast pocket, held it up, then shoved it back into the pocket. Next, he took a small curved knife from his jacket side pocket.

"These weapons are small and handy. Hardly powerful enough to kill anyone, but you can stop an attacker long enough so you can safely get away, provided the other guy doesn't have similar equipment. If someone gets close enough to you, the knife will inflict pain in the sensitive places my colleague described."

Pedro laughed inwardly, not at the absurdity of the situation, but that someone as grossly obese and who talked with such a thick New York accent would use words like "similar equipment," "sensitive," and "colleague."

"On the other hand," Bruno continued, "assuming you don't want him to get that close …"

*Assuming.* Pedro Sanchez chuckled again. Such flowery, articulate language seemed very much out of place, and yet … the guy had said he was sixty-eight, obviously in horrendous shape, but he had *survived* in the world's most vicious jungle.

" … a quick shot to the kneecap or the balls should be enough to do it."

For the next hour, the two thugs, for that's exactly what they were and they made no pretense of being otherwise, entertained and instructed their Hispanic audience with the less savory side, of the business in which they'd been involved for many, many years.

While they had earlier disciplined themselves to the coolness with which they approached their martial arts instruction, they now found themselves opening their minds to a completely different regimen, the art of inflicting pain in the most effective manner.

## PART THREE – CHAPTER 14

"Pedro, do you think we really are becoming men of steel?" Miguel asked that evening.

"Naww," Sanchez cracked. "Maybe Superman or Batman, but if I ever get another hard-on after listening to that lecture this afternoon, I'd prefer it not to be like steel afterward."

"Been awhile, hasn't it, *amigo*?"

"That it has. You know what, Miguel? With everything that's been going on I've been thinking quite a bit about Angie, and not just in the booty department. She really is a good woman in more than just that way. Maybe that's why I want to be something other than just a broke-ass Norteño gang-banger.

"Angie's become a large part of that thought process, not every moment, not every day, but enough. Then there's the little guy. What's he gonna think of his daddy? Or what if it's a little girl? Man, she is going to be the most spoiled brat that ever lived, and if someone like I was ever gets near her …

"You can kill a man by jamming your stiff hand up under his breastbone and tearing his guts, or you can smash his Adam's apple so he strangles. Or you can hit him hard under the nose. That breaks the bone at the bridge of his nose and drives the splinters up into his brain. If a guy like that ever gets close enough to Angelina's and my baby girl …"

Thinking those thoughts, Pedro Sanchez drifted off to sleep.

# 15

"Good morning, gentlemen. You must have been exhausted. It's ten-thirty. I've got good news. First, though, let's have breakfast. Eggs, turkey sausage, hot tea, sweet rolls …"

"No bacon, Mister Imam?" Jorge asked.

"I'm afraid not. We Muslims obey the dietary rules of *halal*. No pork. I passed by your room half an hour after you'd gone to bed. Sounded like you were sawing down a forest, not that there are forests anywhere near Tehachapi."

"Best sleep I can remember, Imam Jarallah. I almost forgot about those guys that kicked us off … I mean those dudes that jumped us and took all our stuff. I hope they rot in hell."

"How many of them were there, Mister Garza?" Jarallah asked mildly, as though he was totally unconcerned with Chuey's answer.

"Must have been forty- …"

"Chuey, you're still in dreamland," Jorge cut in forcefully. "We told the Imam there were *two*."

"Oh, yeah, two," Garza corrected himself. "Just seemed like a bunch more. Maybe that was part of my dream."

While they were hungrily wolfing down breakfast, Jarallah said, "You're really serious about what I said last night? About helping our brothers in the Middle East?"

"Damn straight," Chuey responded. "At least those guys sound like they know what they want and how they're gonna get it. They've got a real direction. Not like this fucked-up country."

"I've got good news for both of you. I spoke to some of the people in our Movement. They talked to some guys who're willing to pony up the money to fly you from L.A. to Istanbul. From there, some other friends will pick you up and drive you to a border crossing into my homeland."

"When do we leave?" Garza asked eagerly.

"Two days from now. That'll give us time to get you passports and visas. One of our people will drive you to L.A. where they'll put you up until the plane is ready to leave."

"Can you get those papers that fast?" Jorge asked suspiciously. "I've heard that takes months."

"Ordinarily you're right," Jarallah said smoothly. "But our friends have friends in high places. We can get these things expedited."

"What kind of stuff do we need to take with us, Imam?" Chuey asked.

"Nothing. The clothes on your back and a carry-on with a couple changes of underwear. Can't have you carrying anything that looks suspicious. We'll give you some money to get by if you need to eat. Our associates will provide the rest."

The "one of our people" turned out to be a very attractive young woman with large dark brown eyes and a hint of generous curves beneath her modest outfit. She drove them to L.A. in a late model Lexus SUV. It became clear to Chuey Garza and Jorge Robles that Imam Jarallah's people were indeed highly placed.

※

"Dennis? Ahmed Jarallah. Two more on the way."

"Did you tag them?"

"Yeah. After I gave them the *spiel* about feeling good about themselves, the lovely women over in Syria, *jihad* fighters getting a free ticket to paradise, seventy-six virgins, four-hundred year orgasms … Baklava, special mint tea, and they were right off to dreamland. I'm sure they never felt a thing. Just like tagging dogs. Gives a new meaning to the word 'dog tags,'" he laughed, "You can trace them anywhere."

"Names?"

"Jésus Garza. Goes by 'Chuey.' Jorge Robles."

"The two guys that got kicked off the bus to Site 51 for knife fighting?" Special Agent O'Brien asked.

"Mmm-hmm. Two of our enforcers called me about nine and told me those bad apples could spoil the whole bunch. I figured they'd probably have the smarts to figure Tehachapi was a lot closer than hoofing it back to Bakersfield, so I hightailed it over. By next morning our little lean-to 'mosque' was all set up. Marielena got a bead on them when they straggled in from the west. When she saw 'em go into McDonald's and start shuffling around some trash that customers had left on the table, she went

## PART THREE – CHAPTER 15

around the back, changed into a burger-flipping outfit, and was waiting for them when they came up to the counter to beg."

"Smart girl, that one. So they're bound to Syria?"

"Yep. They leave Tuesday. Norwegian 7094 to Gatwick. Pegasus 504 to Sabiha Gökçen, arriving 2140 hours. They'll be picked up by a gray Toyota, license 42 RD 3348."

"One of ours?"

"Uh-huh."

Jarallah repeated the tag numbers embedded below the skin in the soft area of Garza's and Robles' lower back. Tags that, within twenty-four hours would not leave the slightest scar.

Two more headed to join up with the bad guys. No need to detail or arrest them. Unknown to Chuey and Jorge, they were now traceable human GPS systems.

When they landed at Istanbul's second airport eighteen hours after they'd taken off from Los Angeles, the young Hispanics found that every passenger under thirty, including themselves, most of the women in headscarves or shawls and most of the men in Tee-shirts or dark sweatshirts, were herded into a closed area. They were lined up in six lanes, three for men, three for women. Chuey and Jorge were the last in their respective lines. They watched as the passports and identifying documents of the people in front of them were scrupulously checked. Then, each person went through a secondary computer investigation. In several cases a woman was taken by another woman into a closed room. Men were similarly sequestered. Emerging half an hour later, they were subjected to pat down searches, handprint, and fingerprint examinations. Garza and Robles, who had never traveled outside the United States before, were becoming very nervous, particularly since more than half of the young passengers were then handcuffed and taken to another area of the airport, beyond their view.

They were third and fourth from the head of the line when a middle-aged man whose skin was slightly lighter than theirs came into the room and spoke briefly with the customs agent in their lane. The agent nodded. The man approached Garza and Robles and crooked his finger, beckoning them to leave the line and follow him. When they hesitated, another customs agent came up to them, shoved them out of the line, and said, in English, "Follow that man, please."

Now thoroughly confused, exhausted, and frightened, they glanced at one another, saw that their choices were limited, and shuffled toward the stranger.

"It's all right," he told them in their own Oaxacan-Mexican dialect. "Sabiha Gökçen is the entry point for the largest percentage of terrorists in the Middle East. The world's intelligence forces watch this airport with special interest, so security is always high here."

"How were you able to get us out of the line?" Jorge asked in English.

The man responded in kind with a two word answer: "Friends. Connections."

"So we're free to leave?"

"As long as you're in my custody."

"Custody? Are we under arrest, Mister …?" This from Chuey.

"In a manner of speaking. My responsibility is to get you to Syria. Imam Jarallah told me when to expect you. We've told them you're United Nations personnel bringing humanitarian aid. Do you have anything other than your carry-on bags?"

At hearing the name of the cleric they'd met back in Tehachapi, Chuey relaxed visibly and said, "Only our bags. You spoke our dialect. How – ?"

"I speak many languages, many dialects," the man answered, switching back to Oaxacan. "Do you prefer yours or English?"

"English, please," said Robles. "Are you Turkish Mister -?"

"Caen, and no, I'm not Turkish."

"Where are you from?"

"The Middle East," he said, breaking into a smile. "Which can mean just about anywhere from Iraq to Persia, all the way down into North Africa. Borders aren't always precise. Meanwhile, I'm sure you fellows are tired. I've booked you a double room at the Boom Palas, only a mile from here. I'll call a cab to drop you off there. Your driver will meet you at ten tomorrow morning."

"It won't be you, Mister Caen?"

"Unfortunately no. I work this airport to ease problems for fellows like you. The Imam is sending others. The room is paid for," he continued. "When you leave the hotel in the morning, there will be a gray Toyota, with Turkish license plate, 42 RD 3348, waiting for you outside the front door. There'll be several other young people in the van who'll be traveling east with you."

As the three men exited the arrivals area, Caen hailed a taxi. "Boom Palas," he told the driver, handing him a wad of Turkish banknotes. Turning back to Garza and Robles he said, "Good luck, gentlemen."

---

"Man, this is one hellaciously big country," Chuey remarked to the young man sitting adjacent to him. The fellow, about his own age, height, and build, wore a tight-fitting black shirt displaying the beret-topped head of the late revolutionary Che Guevara and the words, "Communism killed 100 million people and all I got was this lousy Tee-shirt."

"Yeah," the other answered in a monosyllabic tone that indicated he was not interested in pursuing the conversation further.

The garrulous Chuey persisted. "You from California?"

"Brussels," the man answered, lying back on the headrest.

"No shit? They grow Brussels sprouts in the Salinas Valley. Is Brussels in South County?"

"Belgium," Chuey's seatmate answered. "Brussels is the capital of Belgium." He closed his eyes again, which was just as well because Garza had no desire to betray that he had no idea where, or what, Belgium was.

After they left Istanbul, they skirted the Sea of Marmara as far as Kocaeli, then climbed into beautiful mountainous vistas as they approached Bolu. Four hours later, they reached Ataturk's capital city, Ankara, in the midst of dry, dusty hills. Turning south, they drove to the east of Tüzgolu, Turkey's great salt lake, and continued into higher mountain country, until they came to a tent city north of Adana, ten miles from the huge American air base.

## PART THREE – CHAPTER 15

"We'll catch a good night's sleep here," the driver said. "Tomorrow morning you'll get a glimpse of what'll be your new home for awhile." He did not say how long 'awhile' would be.

Next day, Jorge Robles met the driver in the communal garage and repair shop where the Toyota had been housed overnight. Their driver seemed to be poring over a large wall map of the area. It appeared to be a short drive down to Hatay, then across the border into Aleppo, until recently Syria's largest city.

"Shouldn't take us long to get there," Jorge mentioned to their chauffeur.

"Ordinarily you'd be right, my young friend," he said. "But this is wartime. Everyone who can do so is getting *out* of the city. It would be hard to deliver aid *to* Aleppo when no one seems to want to stay there."

"So where will we go?"

"East to Şanliurfa, a four hour drive if we're lucky. Another forty-five minutes south to Akçakale, just over the border from Tell Abyad, Syria. We'll drop you off there. Your friends will take you from Tell Abyad to Al-Raqqah, your final destination."

"I thought we'd be going to Damascus," Jorge said.

"Nope. That's Assad's stronghold. I thought you guys wanted to fight Mister Assad."

"Oh, right," Robles said. "This Al Rocka, is he the guy we're going to meet up with?"

"You could say that," the driver replied. "Why don't you go get some breakfast before we take off?"

# 16

"**Well,** Generalissimo Tommy, time to begin our great adventure. Next Monday we head for the land Down Under. You must be thrilled about getting back in the game."

"Well, uh ... Field Marshal ... uh ... Sister ..."

"Maureen, Tommy. It's been months. We've been on a first-name basis since the second time we met."

"Yes, but this is different. I don't quite know how to say this ... that is ... can we meet somewhere in private, just you and me ... uh ...?"

"Is something wrong, Tommy?"

"No, uh ... yes ... I mean ..."

"You name the time and the place and I'll be there."

"I'd really appreciate if you could keep this under your hat, Sister ..."

"Maureen, Tommy. How many times do I have to tell you that?"

"Yeah, but just for this conversation, uh, *confession*, I'd like, well, you know ..."

"Of course, my friend. How about a walk at Point Lobos?" she said, naming a stunning spit of forested land stretching into the Pacific Ocean just south of the Monterey Peninsula. "The walk would do us both good."

※

"Now, Tommy, what was it you wanted to talk about so urgently?"

"I don't know that I can do this, Sister."

This time she didn't bother to correct him.

"I'm listening," she said mildly.

"Well, uh, you know almost everything there is to know about my past life."

"That's so."

"I was pretty active on the East Coast back in the day."

"Including that little stretch of time at Allentown. I imagine your name was known over a good part of the underworld."

"Yeah, Sister. My *name* was well known. But the problem is, they always came to me. Sister, I'm scared shitless. I've never set foot outside this country. I wouldn't know the first thing to do. I've never had a passport in my life. I don't know any foreign language except maybe New York Sicilian. I haven't the slightest idea what to do or say."

"*You*, the *Capo de Capi*, the boss of bosses? Surely you've been to Sicily? To Italy? To the Vatican, for God's sake?"

"Afraid not, Sister Maureen. We're supposed to start on this ... this *thing* next week and I was too ashamed to tell you, too embarrassed to ask anyone how you even go about doing this."

"But we were together in the Turkish Republic of Northern Cyprus over a month ago."

"Yeah, but I didn't need a passport, everything was arranged. I didn't have to do a thing. Just a group of old guys like me and one of you. It was no different than a bunch of us getting together in the Poconos."

Sister Maureen chuckled good-naturedly. "Tommy, there's nothing to be afraid of. We're on unofficial 'official' business. I'll go you one better by making sure you're several steps up from an ordinary passport. I'll have a diplomatic passport for you in any name you want within two days."

"What's the difference between a regular passport and a diplomatic passport?"

"The diplomatic passport's your best-ever friend in high places. You don't wait in line anywhere, you can't be arrested. They won't even give you a parking ticket if you park overnight in a red zone."

"That all sounds great, Sister Maureen. But there is one more thing."

"Yes, Generalissimo?"

"I'm … uh … that is … I'm scared shitless of flying."

"Oh, Tommy," she burst out, but kindly. "Don't you remember that long, long flight to TRNC?"

"Not really, Sister Maureen. I'd taken two sleeping pills and a great deal of Scotch, and I was flat out on my ass from twenty minutes after we took off until ten minutes before we landed. L.A.'s a piece of cake. Washington or New York's stretching it. But Australia? How long a flight is that?"

"Fifteen hours, plus or minus."

"Way too damn long, Sister. I'll crap my pants or spew my insides out in that time. Probably die in the process."

"Tommy, you'll just have to show me how big and brave you are. I'll sit next to you and hold your hand if necessary the whole way."

"I don't think you'll be able to guarantee that, Maureen."

"What makes you think I won't?"

"Please pardon me for saying this, Sister, but the airlines have gotten so damn greedy that they're now making you pay extra if you want a particular seat and want to sit next to a friend or family member."

"I think our great and good government may spring for that charge."

The man who emerged at Melbourne's Terminal 2 a week later was unrecognizable as the same elderly fellow who, only a week before, had shambled uncertainly and quivered in fear before the tiny nun. He'd shed ten years and displayed a spring to his step akin to his swagger of forty years earlier. He was attired in a trim-fitting, expensive cut suit of the finest quality. His shoes were buffed to a high gloss. He'd transformed into the *Capo di Capi* of his halcyon salad days.

"Well?" Sister Maureen Richards inquired. "That wasn't so bad, was it?"

"Not at all, Field Marshal. That was one monster sonofabitch airplane. Not one bump. That baby must have sat on the sky and mashed down any turbulence. You know, Sister Maureen, maybe I could learn to fly one of those."

"That might just be a little presumptuous Tommy. The Airbus 380 is nearly twice as big as the 747. If you want to buy one, all you need to do is write out a little check for 433 million dollars."

"Okay, I guess I'll settle for a 747," Aiello remarked casually. "Now where the hell is this Simpson Desert?"

"Three days' drive to Birdsville."

"Birdsville?" What the hell kind of name is that for a city?"

"Hey, Don Aiello, a little respect, please," Sister Maureen replied. "The population of the metropolis of the Simpson Desert is just under 200. It once had three hotels, two stores, a customs house for interstate trade, a police station and a lot of commercial buildings. Today just one hotel survives, but you can get canned or bottled beer, read a book in the library, or take in the visitor information center."

"I'm impressed," Aiello said caustically. "How long will boys spend in advanced training?"

"Three weeks. Hopefully they won't go entirely crazy."

"How many we got?"

"Twenty thousand. The desert's two hundred fifty miles wide by two hundred miles long, so there'll never be more than five hundred men within lots of miles of one another. We've set up forty campsites at strategic points throughout the desert. Tents only, no buildings. No water except what we carry in. You want to go to the bathroom, you dig a hole in the sand. After you've gone, you cover it up."

"How long before we put the first ones in-country?"

"A month."

## PART THREE – CHAPTER 16

"What're they supposed to learn out here?"

"Only two things, Tommy. How to kill and how to avoid being killed."

Two weeks later, ten C-5A Galaxy Military Transport aircraft a day started landing at Alice Springs Regional Airport, five hundred miles from nowhere, courtesy of the United States Air Force. Each of these monsters carried 300 troops plus three weeks' worth of supplies, tents, equipment, water purifiers, food, and clothing. The plan was to leave supplies for later recruits once the first training classes were sent to that amorphous place called "the front." Alice Springs' 7,999-foot-long runway 12/30 was more than ample to accommodate the transports. Within a week, the first 20,000 volunteers had landed and been bussed from "The Alice," to Birdsville, 1,150 miles and 24 hours' drive away, then dispersed into the vast desert.

The fourteen generals, one generalissimo, and one small nun took up headquarters at the Birdsville hotel, which, despite its plain Jane exterior, was, by Outback standards, luxurious. They'd planned to stay in the Simpson Desert for the first three weeks to ensure that everything was running smoothly. Then the advanced training would be turned over to their trusted subordinates. The leadership would move considerably closer to the operations theater.

"I thought they said the desert is the hottest place on earth," Pedro said. "I've never experienced such cold in all my life."

His friend Miguel and others noticed, and mentioned to others, that during the past two months Sanchez's vocabulary had become quite different than when he'd boarded the bus at the Salinas Greyhound station. He seemed to express his ideas more directly and more eloquently than in the past. Miguel noted that Pedro had taken to reading dictionaries and pronouncing new words during down time.

Pedro's trainers had also written in his effectiveness reports, which they never disclosed either to him or to others, that Sanchez displayed valuable traits which pointed to him becoming a platoon leader, maybe more, in their ranks.

Pedro himself hardly noticed these changes. He spent a great deal of what free time there was emailing Angie. His messages contained suggestions of how they might cement their future if, when, he made it home from his duties. He encouraged her to finish school and let her know that she was free to draw on an account which had been opened in his name at the East Alisal branch of Chase Bank. He notified the bank to add her as a signator to the account (he didn't even know what that meant the day he left Salinas, but he'd learned things quickly).

Angie was shocked, a bit frightened, and certainly proud of the change that had come over her man. She sent him selfies at his new email address and wrote that she was doing fine; that she had gone over to Natividad Hospital for a checkup; and that she might take up a job as an orderly at the hospital, which paid way better than what she was now earning.

One of the selfies showed her with another man, which momentarily piqued Pedro's jealousy until he saw that the man in the picture was Alejandro Villarreal. The second selfie quickly quenched his hot feelings when he saw that it portrayed the three of them, Angie, Alejandro, and his buddy's fiancée, Sarita.

## PART THREE – CHAPTER 16

"Thirty-seven degrees last night," Miguel said. "Feels like it's even colder tonight."

"I recall reading that it got up to 122° in the summer. It's now the beginning of June, so where's the heat?"

"Up in the northern hemisphere," Miguel replied. "Don't forget, the seasons are reversed down here. It only gets to be about 60 during the day."

"Do you think the guys at the top gave any thought that we'd be going to wherever the hell we're going in the middle of summer?" Pedro muttered.

"I'm sure they did. It would be kinda' risky if we suddenly dropped out of the sky into the neighborhood and started killing people."

There'd been no letup in their conditioning regimen, but now the trainees learned the strategy and tactics of guerilla warfare. Most of their post-exercise physical training took place at night. They'd been doled out Yukon NV 1x24 night vision goggles two days after their arrival. Learning to use them was a chore, but once they got used to the unreality of infrared lighting up the darkest night, they realized how necessary they would be when they were in the strange, forbidding atmosphere of the Middle East. As the first week blended into the second and the third week came at them with incredible speed, the troops' readiness for action and the tight bonding of esprit de corps became very real. The difference between life and death might very well depend on "I've got your back." During the final week, the recruits ultimately coalesced into cells of three men each, fireteams. Four fireteams equaled a squad, three squads a platoon, twenty thousand a division. It all looked nice and orderly on a chart, but in real life it was you and two other guys.

By the end of the third week, twenty thousand volunteers were more than ready to go. All they worried about was how they'd be dropped *into* two countries from which people were *leaving* in droves without anyone realizing they had arrived.

They had no doubt that someone smarter than they had made the decision. Somehow they felt comforted knowing that God was their leader, in the person of a small retired nun.

# 17

"**Manucher,** I need a very small favor from you which will translate into a very big favor for your government."

"I'm listening, Ezra."

"Your guys like Assad. The U.S. doesn't like Assad. Your guys know what a pain in the ass ISIS is. The U.S. knows what a pain in the ass ISIS is. Although there's enough meat on the carcass for both of us to eat, we've got to kill the lamb before we feast."

"The enemy of my enemy is my friend. Politics makes very strange bedfellows."

"We need to get twenty thousand young men into ISIS country."

"We?"

"The Vatican."

"The *what*?"

"Because of the somewhat unorthodox activity we've planned, the good, moral, U.S. of A. cannot be involved in this …"

As Ezra Caen told his Iranian "good guy" equivalent all the details, the Persian spymaster laughed incredulously. "That's the absolutely ultimate in *chutzpah!*"

"It's pronounced *khutz-pah*, Manucher, like gargling. Not *hutz-pah* or *tschutz-pah*. You'll never make it as a Jew."

"Ezra, I never wanted to be more than a *sheygetz* and a Muslim *sheygetz* at that."

"We've got a whole fleet of old C-5A Galaxies, big mamas, bigger than a 747. We can't ask Syria or Iraq to let us use their bases or civilian airports to offload these guys. It would look a little obvious and the enemy *du jour* would go apeshit."

"Anything that could identify these aircraft as U.S.?"

"Nothing that could identify them as anything. Flat gray. Not a single mark anywhere. The troops won't be wearing anything but street clothes. Their instructions are to disperse all over ISIS-land the minute they get off the plane."

"Iran won't be the only point of entry?"

"Nope. They'll be coming in from ten different directions. Incirlik is an obvious embarkation point, so the smallest contingent will land there. A lot more will be deplaning at *Selah Shalom* airbase in the Negev. The Saudis, the Turks, the Egyptians, and the Kuwaitis are on board. Jordan's the most upset of all since they beheaded a Jordanian fighter pilot. The Jordanians flew more sorties against ISIS than anyone except the U.S. Lebanon's not so eager 'cause it's in harm's way, but it's agreed to let one plane a week in for exactly as long as it takes to unload it and get the hell out."

"How many aircraft would you want to land in the Islamic Republic, Ezra?"

## PART THREE – CHAPTER 17

"One or two a day."

"Who takes 'em to the frontier?"

"Rouhani's government won't have to worry about that. The old generals have their own way of dealing with logistics."

"How long do you expect this operation to last?"

"Until they get the job done."

"All right, gentlemen, time to get our ducks in a row," Sister Maureen commanded. They occupied a large meeting room in the Dan Hotel, halfway between Tel Aviv and Haifa. As was so common here, the Israelis had mastered security, always the largest problem in the part of the world, down to a science. She flipped the computer on to a power point presentation on a large screen.

"There are fourteen of you. No sense in any of you setting foot inside the war zone unless absolutely necessary. The enemy is focused for the most part in eastern Syria and northwest Iraq. Mosul in Iraq and Al-Raqqah in Syria are their capitals. Notice the country with the longest border abutting each of them."

"Turkey," said 'Generalissimo' Aiello.

"Nominally a friendly state. Realistically, the Turks'll play both ends against the middle so long as the Kurds are squashed in between. The Erdoğan government is upset with everyone nowadays. The U.S. glorifies the Kurds as heroes on the front line against the Islamic State, which is exactly what the Turks do *not* want to hear. But the Turkish government has decided to renew old enmities with the Russian bear, whom they hate even more than they detest the Kurds, Putin's embracing Bashar al-Assad, whom they don't like either. Over two million refugees have camped on the border just inside Turkey."

"One royally screwed up place," an octogenarian said. He walked over to a pitcher of lemon-scented water and poured a glass for himself.

"It's a very long and very crowded gathering place," Sister Maureen continued. "Iraq's longest border of all is with Iran, not the most conducive place to be, but our Israeli friend," she nodded at Ezra Caen, "seems to have the best connection there. Probably because we're the 'Great Satan,' and Israel's only the 'Little Satan.'"

Laughter filled the room.

"No border with Syria, but passage between Syria and Iraq is very fluid and easy in ISIS-land. Jordan borders both Iraq and Syria. They aren't happy to have the Islamic State on their doorstep. They're loyal to the United States and they rely on Israel to give them some sense of security. They haven't got much choice when it comes to keeping ISIS out, but so far the Islamic State stays pretty much to the north and east of the Hashemite Kingdom."

"Not to mention they've got a queen who's one the most gorgeous women alive," tiny boss Gigante said."

"Yeah, and you'd get lost inside her, Midget," the Philadelphia Don quipped good naturedly.

"Oh, I don't know," Gigante replied. "I sure would let you have the other seventy-five virgins in exchange for Her Majesty. By the way, there's a great buffet on the table over there, and while we're dreaming about …"

"Generals, should I be listening to this kind of talk?" Sister Maureen asked.

"The two retired *Capos* blushed and walked over to the buffet together. Each piled his plate high with eggplant, spinach, salmon, turkey, falafel, and fruit salad.

The rest of the men followed suit. Two white-jacketed waiters poured water and the diner's choice of white or red wine. Maureen passed out miniatures of the Middle East map that she'd shown on the large screen to each of the men.

Earlier, they had worked together to divide the Iraq-Syria zone into sectors. While the troops had rigorously been training, physically and mentally, the old *dons* had done their homework as well. Now, each worked together to find the closest safe haven to their own sector. Six of them selected stations along the Turkish frontier, three chose positions inside Iran. Two picked Jordan, two more decided on Saudi Arabia, and the final general put his index finger over Kuwait. "I'll simply live at Al-Mubarak Air Base," he said. "It's clean, modern, civilized, and comfortable. How about you, Sister?" he asked their Field Marshal.

"The Holy Land, where else?" she responded, crossing herself. "Okay, my friends, now that we've divided things up, here's a list for each of you showing where your troops will land, and when. Your job is to get them to where they need to be. You tell us what you need to get them there, we'll handle that part, and the rest is up to you. While you've been studying the 'big picture,' we've worked with your adjutants and they've come up with lists of the most promising recruits."

After Sister Maureen passed out these lists, she said, "Your soldiers will arrive between three days and two weeks from now. You should meet every one of them when they land. Twenty thousand is a pretty good start. That's a lot of chess pieces on the board and it's up to you guys to move them around to best advantage. Don Aiello and I will be roving the area and visiting each of you at your headquarters. Any questions?"

"What about weapons, Sister?" a spry lad of seventy asked.

"They'll be on the plane that's bringing them in. You'll have to figure a way to get them in-country. No one's ever underestimated the power of *baksheesh* (bribery) in this part of the world. I'll stay around for as long as you need me to answer any other concerns you might have. One last thing. Each of you will get several thousand golf balls coming in on each flight."

"Balls, Sister?" one of the Dons asked.

"Calling cards, General DiCavalcante," Sister Maureen replied.

"Calling cards? Now I'm more confused than ever," the retired *Capo* said.

"Gino, come over to the dessert area with me. Would you like tea or coffee?"

"Coffee, please. But I'd really like to know what this balls, calling card sh– ... stuff is all about."

"Do you want to walk over to the dessert table with me or not?"

As the two of them walked together, Sister Maureen Richards talked very softly to her subordinate, who had a long-deserved reputation as one of the most bloodthirsty killers in any family.

*Don* Gino DiCalvacante blushed. Very very red.

As they returned, Sister Maureen, carrying a china teacup in one hand and a piece baklava on a matching plate, asked, in a normal voice, "Do you have any preference which color you want for your sector, General?"

"Of course, Sister. Brass."

"Mister Tabrizi, I'm so glad to meet you. Ezra Caen couldn't say enough good things about you, starting with how you saved his life during the Assassin caper."

"Hardly a caper, Sister Maureen," the Iranian said. "He covered my back and I covered his. The end of the Ahmadinejad days, the beginning of Rouhani's tenure."

"It was kind of you to come to Turkey. I appreciate even more that you've arranged lodgings for three of our leaders in the Islamic Republic during the operation. Was it much trouble?"

"Not at all, Sister. It made it much easier when I disclosed that they weren't Americans. I must say, even though they had Vatican passports they certainly didn't look like 'men of the cloth,' nor did they appear to be high-ranking ambassadors. More like well-dressed thugs. It's a good thing no one questions a diplomatic passport."

"That's for sure, Mister Tabrizi." They were seated at an outside *lokanta* in Iskenderun, historic Alexandria at the eastern end of the Mediterranean. As usual, Turkish cuisine was ample and delicious.

"Orūmīyeh was an obvious choice, since it's the closest Persian city to Mosul. Īlām's close to Baghdad, which is not near the ISIS-controlled area. Ahvāz is farther south, but perfect for your troops to come up through Iraq's underbelly and encircle the bad guys. When does the operation start?"

She smiled ambiguously. "Any day now."

Tabrizi lifted his glass of tea. "*Şerefinize!* To your health!"

"*Bol Şanslar!*" she responded in Turkish. "Good luck to all of us. God knows we may need it."

*Part Four*

***GAME ON***

# 18

EIGHT clicks outside the city. Might as well be a thousand miles away. No wind. Quiet except for the night sounds. Rats. Mice. Probably snakes, too. Who cared?Perimeter guards slouched, outside the compound. Bored. Same old same old every night. Even the Black Standard, the *Jihadist* flag attached to a stanchion to the right of the nearest guard, Abu Omar al-Mosli, drooped forlornly.

Al-Mosli slipped to a sitting position on the ground. His chin had just dropped to his chest. His eyes closed. He'd barely started snoring when he felt his neck caught in a viselike grip and his body roughly pulled to its feet. Before he could even muster a surprised grunt, he felt the cold edge of a curved knife gently drawn across his neck, hardly breaking the skin, and he heard the soft menacing voice in Levant-accented Arabic."Not a word, *al'abalah, tafahhum?*" As al-Mosli started to choke out an obscenity, the sinister voice continued, "They told me that when you *jihad al'awghad* die in a holy war you each get seventy-two virgins to play with and four-hundred-year orgasms. Maybe, maybe not, *raghead*, but you'll need to have *cojones* to do anything with those ladies, and balls you will not have, *tafahhum?*" The guard stifled a gasp.

Scarcely a moment later, while the attacker kept a chokehold on al-Mosli's neck, the hand holding the knife descended. Two swift strokes and the now-neutered *jihadi* writhed on the ground, moaning in ultimate agony as his assailant departed and moved silently into the darkness.

"On second thought, *castrati*, I should leave you with a couple of balls." The Hispanic American took two orange golf balls from his rucksack and placed them gently on the ground next to his victim.

❧

"A chain saw? That's truly ugly, *muchacho*."

"They said we should use whatever tools we take from the bad guys. Before I took it from him, he had sliced off that poor woman's …"

His mate turned his head away in disgust, then steeled himself to life on the ground as it existed now. They were not here to play party games and pass around doughnuts. Yes, these guys were human beings, just like him. They had wives, sisters, daughters … But why would one human being mutilate another for no other reason than because the other human being didn't agree with the way *he* lived?

"You think they wouldn't do the same to *your* girlfriend? You think they wouldn't cut *your* balls off if you came into their territory? I know it sickens you, *amigo*. Don't think I didn't vomit the first dozen times. As hard as it is for me to do this, 'cause I consider myself a decent human being, what choice do we have? The general told us it's like cancer. If you leave it alone, it spreads and kills even more people."

"Yeah, yeah, I know, Gustavo. But there are times …"

"Rodrigo, how'd you like to be a cancer doctor and tell the family that dad's got six months to live, and he'll just slowly slide downhill getting weaker and more helpless every day?"

"Man, these desert nights are so quiet, you can hear every sound. And look at those stars. Never saw anything like that back in L.A. Wonder what the people on those stars are thinking?"

"What makes you think people live on those stars, Rodrigo?"

"I imagine people must live somewhere. Maybe if they do live up there they can see us."

"They'd have to have awfully big, powerful telescopes my friend. I …"

That was the last sound either young man ever heard. They didn't feel their necks being severed, nor did they know that their killers had carved huge crosses in their bodies from neck to lower torso and across their breastbones, until their insides spilled out onto the desert sand.

The sun set. Pedro headed down and around the rise, moving slowly from bush to bush. The countryside to the east was low. It did not appear to have seen much fighting. He saw lights on a hill to the east. *Dear God, let them be our guys*, he prayed silently.

He was halfway across the valley when he heard a shuffling sound. More rats? He didn't know. The sound became louder. As he turned, Pedro saw a man running toward him. The stranger's rifle was raised, the bayonet aimed at him.

His first thought was, "Christ, don't let me die!" The next was, "Don't let him be one of ours!" He spun round, dove for the ground, and dodged as the other man swiped at him. He ripped a dagger from his belt and struck at the back of the man's leg. With a shocked scream, his assailant went down. No time to think. Pedro struck again and again, plunging his dagger into soft flesh wherever he could find it. The man's body convulsed, then collapsed in a heap.

When Pedro finally recovered enough to stop stabbing, his hand was wet and sticky. The other man gurgled. Pedro's eyes became accustomed to the dark. His attacker wouldn't be getting up again. Bile churned in his throat. He lurched a few yards from the dying man and retched until he felt his insides would come out. He still didn't know if his assailant was an Assad supporter, an ISIS crazy, a Kurd, or some other kind of fighter. Was he alone? If he wasn't, Pedro knew that anyone within fifty yards would have heard the scuffle. He found a shallow burrow, twenty feet from where the man lay, and waited.

Twenty minutes went by. The man continued to emit a bubbling noise as he strained to breathe. Pedro tried to cover his ears to blot out the horrible sound. When he did, he noticed his own head was wet. Putting his fingers to his lips, he tasted blood. Odd, he didn't feel particularly weak. Instinctively, he grabbed for some dirt and rubbed it against his head. Probably just grazed by the bayonet. Then realization hit. An inch either way and he would be the one gurgling in his death throes, not the other man.

An hour passed. The bubbling sound had become a dry rasp. The man was dying. Pedro crawled over, possessed by morbid curiosity. The other, he was wearing a green camouflage uniform, an "Afghani robe," which Pedro had learned was one of five distinctive outfits worn by Islamic State warriors, opened his eyes and stared at him with a look of utter terror. His body lay still, silent. His eyes confronted Pedro with an expression the young soldier would never forget. Resignation? Accusation? Anger?

The dying man worked his mouth half open and tried to speak. No sound came. Pedro stared back at him. The overwhelming magnitude of what he'd done struck home. This was not a nameless, faceless enemy. Not like shooting across a vast field, tossing a grenade into an enemy concentration. Not even the same as seeing his comrades fall. He was witnessing the death of another human being, a death he had caused. Pedro moved closer. With superhuman effort, the man tried to say something. Nothing came out.

Pedro reached for his canteen and opened it. Only a few drops of water left. They'd be wasted on a dead man. He looked at the other man's face again. The look was helpless, condemning. Pedro poured the last few drops onto the sleeve of his tunic. He pressed the moistened sleeve against the dying man's mouth. The eyes ceased their anger and became softer.

"May your Allah bless you," Pedro said softly. Were the man's eyes actually forgiving? Pedro never knew. A moment later they were sightless. The man was dead.

Pedro felt a chill. His face was wet, but now the wetness was from tears, not blood. An hour ago, a moment ago, this man had lived, breathed, spoken with his comrades, even joked with them. After all, as insane with bloodlust as he'd been taught these lunatics were, every one of them was no less a human being than he was. Who knows what life events had brought the man he had killed to join the Islamic State? Praise God, he'd killed an ISIS warrior. At least it was the enemy. Did he have a wife? A mother? Was he any less of a man because he was fighting under a different set of generals? For different leaders?

Pedro rolled the corpse over and saw a wallet in the man's back pocket. He removed it with trembling hands. Two pictures and a letter fell out. A quarter-moon had risen in the night sky. Pedro hadn't even noticed it before. No wonder it had been so easy to see the man's eyes. He couldn't read the strange lettering on the envelope. There were two photographs. A small woman with a serious face, wearing a headscarf, stood alone in the first one. In the second, she was flanked on each side by a little girl, each with braided hair. The man's daughters? Pedro felt like a dagger had been thrust into his chest.

There was an identity card written in Arabic and in English. It identified the dead man as Abu al-Nasr, twenty-six, poet and school teacher. Pedro wept openly and vomited what little remained inside of him.

"How many down?" Sister Maureen asked, opening the meeting. She and Tommy Aiello had arranged a conference with their fourteen Lieutenant-Generals, Ezra Caen, Manucher Tabrizi, and Dennis O'Brien, in a private meeting room of the Kubbeli Lounge in Istanbul's Pera Palas Jumeira Hotel.

It was not without purpose that Sister Maureen had chosen this particular venue. What was then known simply as the *Pera Palas*, had originally been built in 1892. George Nagelmackers, the founder of *Wagons Lits*, had built it in the heart of *European* Istanbul because he didn't think there was a place luxurious enough for his Grand European Express. In its heyday, it had housed kings and prime ministers, actors and whores. Ernest Hemingway had stayed there for long periods. Agatha Christie had written her masterpiece, *Murder on the Orient Express,* there. Kemal Atatürk, the father of modern Turkey, expressly reserved Room 101 for his personal use.

Closed in 2006, the historic icon, which in the 1960s had sunk to a level where it had been an entry in Arthur Frommer's *Europe on Five Dollars a Day*, had been completely restored and reopened as a "museum-hotel" in 2010. Today, the cheapest of its 115 rooms started at $350 a night.

"We've used over 7,500 balls," Tommy replied.

"There's bound to have been some duplication," Ezra said. "Do you have a closer estimate?"

"At least five thousand during the three months since the operation started," Aiello responded.

"How many of ours?" Sister Maureen pressed.

"Again, and it's only an estimate from our sector leaders, a little less than a thousand."

"Agent O'Brien, does the FBI have any reliable figures on how many supporters or soldiers the Islamic State has recruited in the last three months?"

"Seventy-five hundred, give or take a couple thousand."

"Either way, that's not the way it was supposed to be, gentlemen," the Field Marshal said. "I had hoped we would be well on our way to wiping them out by now."

"Sister," Ezra Caen said quietly. "Dennis's idea was a good one, and it's still a good one. But if your, our, goal was to completely destroy every single ISIS sympathizer and member, that's an impossible dream. You Americans were ecstatic when you caught and killed Osama Bin Laden. Did that destroy Al-Qaeda? It did not. It simply caused what remained of that movement to split into different factions, one of which became the Islamic State."

"My friends," Tabrizi added. "As long as human nature is the way it has always been, there will always be conflict, sometimes

## PART FOUR – CHAPTER 18

within accepted bounds of what people call 'civilized behavior,' but when someone wants something badly enough it escalates in a different direction. Case in point, what some people call 'ethnic cleansing' others call 'genocide.' Sixty years ago, Nelson Mandela, Menachem Begin, and God knows how many others were 'terrorists.' Today they're revered as 'freedom fighters' or even 'statesmen.'"

"So you're saying we'll never be able to do the job we came to do?" Aiello asked sadly.

"I don't think that's quite what my Persian friend meant," Ezra responded. "Thirty-five years ago, the world discovered a terrifying new epidemic, AIDS. It was a one-way ticket to death. We believed no one would ever stop it and the world population would be decimated, much as it had been during the influenza pandemic that spread after World War I. Were either of these diseases completely eradicated?"

"Eradicated? What does that word mean, Mister Caen?"

"Signor Riina, I'm sorry I got up on my high horse with fancy language," Ezra replied. "It means exactly what Sister Maureen said, 'wiped out.' And no, the flu was not wiped out and AIDS was not wiped out, and cancer was not wiped out, and war has never been wiped out. But sooner or later the world moves on. Things adjust. Things change. People don't change. But events change their options."

Special Agent O'Brien, who'd been gazing out the window of their conference room overlooking the magnificent Golden Horn and the historical old city which had once ruled the known world, turned back to the meeting.

"Mister Caen is absolutely right," he said. "Some years ago I read a novel that took place in Switzerland in the Middle Ages.

The Helvetii, which the Romans called the Swiss in an earlier day, had been warlike, but somewhere along the line they decided to be completely neutral. Instead of taking part in a war, the Swiss would stand on the sidelines and sell arms and everything else they could to *both* sides. Switzerland, which, by that time, was a Christian country, got very, very rich doing that.

"One of the characters in the book attended the swearing-in of Basel's new head Priest. He publicly asked the recently-ordained clergyman, who'd previously been the town's wealthiest merchant, 'Dear Father, how do you reconcile your Christian principles with the fact that this city owes so much of its prosperity to the perpetual waging of war between nations? Will you preach against that?'

"'I will not!' the priest snapped. 'Christianity does not forbid the making of war, so long as it is a *just* war. Since every war has its end in peace, and since peace is a divine blessing, then every war can be called just.'"

Sister Maureen's eyes and her mouth opened wide, but she said nothing.

"When I read that," the FBI agent continued, "I thought that was a most *un-Christian* and cynical statement. But then I learned that during the Iran-Contra fiasco and the Iran-Iraq war, that's exactly what the U.S., the Soviet Union, and every other 'moral' country that could profit from those adventures was doing. It's the way of the world."

All of the Dons at the meeting started talking at once. Some were outraged, some were frankly confused. Many believed they'd been hoodwinked into this adventure, which they surmised was now doomed to failure, that they were only pawns in a cosmic chess game among countries and movements larger and more powerful than they were.

## PART FOUR – CHAPTER 18

"Mister FBI bigshot, are you saying we've been bought off to do your dirty work?" the smallest and oldest of the mobsters, Mario Gigante, accused.

"Not at all, Don Gigante," O'Brien replied. "Remember what Mister Caen just said? 'War has never been wiped out. But sooner or later the world moves on. Things adjust. Things change. People don't change. But events change their options.' What you gentlemen are doing is what diplomats, warriors, and world leaders have done since the beginning of time. *You are creating the events that will change options in this part of the world*. Boots on the ground haven't done it. Airstrikes haven't done it. Billions of dollars haven't done it. But you guys, and the 'soldiers' under you *are* doing it.

"Most of the leaders of the Islamic State and their followers are less than half your age. They're physically strong, they're terrorizing the world, and every one of them individually has got more piss and vinegar than the whole bunch of you put together. So how do you fight that? By your own experiences. Simply by remembering that *old age and treachery will defeat youth and vigor every time*."

"Gentlemen," Sister Maureen said quietly. "I think it's time for us to discuss a program to drive home our point with some rather dramatic events."

At the end of the meeting, the attendees dispersed back to whence they'd come.

Smiling.

# 19

AT the same moment that the huge C-5A loaded with the latest batch of the Wrecking Crew entered Turkish airspace on its way to the American Air Base at Incirlik, a venerable Grumman Gulfstream II passed above the military aircraft at 35,000 feet, continuing eastward over the Mediterranean, en route from Charleroi-Brussels airport toward Baghdad. Abu Safwan al-Rifai, Subcommander of the Islamic State's Security and Intelligence Council, the sole passenger on the private jet, had slipped his loafers off, relaxed, and was thinking how fortunate he'd been since he'd changed allegiances from Saddam Hussein's Baathist Party to his current employer. The Iraqi, now a top member of the powerful Council, was responsible for removing threats, both to the Caliph and the Islamic State, through assassinations, largely of defectors and challengers to the regime.

A reedy voice came over Grumman's speakers in fluid Levantine Arabic, *"As-salamu alaykum, takrim alssayr al-Rifai,"* Allah's blessing be upon you. I'm dreadfully sorry about the slight delay. If you look out the porthole to your right, you'll see we're just making landfall. Baghdad Tower has cleared us to land. We should be on the ground by ten-thirty local time.

# PART FOUR – CHAPTER 19

Please set your chronometer forward if you've not already done so. Thank you for your patience. Please sit back and enjoy the rest of the flight."

Al-Rifai glanced down at his left wrist and prepared to adjust his watch ahead. The timepiece showed eight-seventeen, Greenwich Mean Time. His last conscious thought as the explosion ripped through the plane, killing both the subcommander and his pilot was, "This cannot be happening. Not now. Not when life is so very good."

The only segment of the aircraft large enough to be readily identified two days later was the tail. There was a large blue golf ball painted on each side.

※

Abdulla Ahmad al-Mishhadani looked at the clock on the wall of Baghdad International Airport. Twelve-fifteen. The Turkish Airlines flight from Istanbul was due in half an hour. The board showed that Flight 302 would be arriving on time. The last two nights had been sleepless ones, but given his position in the hierarchy he had to put on his most exuberant and welcoming face for the new arrivals.

Al-Mishhadani was the Islamic State's logistics expert. His job among the ISIS leadership was one where joy alternated with sadness every day. On the one hand, when foreign fighters arrived from around the world, al-Mishhadani made sure they had a place to stay. On the other, he was responsible for transporting the Army's suicide bombers to their target locations.

"Abdulla Ahmad al-Mishhadani, Honorable Abdulla Ahmad al-Mishhadani, please pick up the nearest red courtesy telephone. Abdulla Ahmad al-Mishhadani, red courtesy telephone please."

*Allah is great, Allah is good, what kind of fuckup is there now?* He thought grumpily as he approached the airport courtesy phone forty feet away.

He'd gotten halfway to his destination when a small, swarthy man in his late twenties, most likely a Lebanese or Iranian tourist by his dress, addressed him courteously "Excuse me, Sir, have you the time?"

"Of course." Al-Mishhadani snapped, raising his left arm and twisting his wrist to look at his watch. It was the last move he ever made. By the time the Airport security police had discovered the tiny needle mark in al-Mishhadani's side, the only thing of an unusual nature they found were two purple golf balls, one in each of his front pockets.

Khairy Abed Mahmoud al-Taey, a member of the Military Council, felt incredibly honored to have been selected to lead a small delegation to Pyongyang. Normally he was in charge of the placement and deployment of IEDs, Improvised Explosive Devices, roadside bombs. In the second Iraq War, IEDs were used extensively against U.S.-led invasion forces. By the end of 2007 they had been responsible for 63% of coalition deaths in Iraq.

On the evening of his third and last day in the North Korean capital, he'd successfully concluded negotiations with delegates sent by Premier Pak Pong-ju and parliamentary chairman Kim Yong-nam, second and third only to Kim Jong-un himself. True, he'd never personally met with any of these men, but the fact that they'd sent an official delegation to meet with him meant that the North Korean superpower recognized the Islamic State as a worthy brother in the community of nations.

## PART FOUR – CHAPTER 19

Al-Taey's rising star in the Caliphate would be assured when the leadership learned he'd arranged for a shipment of almost one ton of advanced detonating devices and explosives which would shortly be used against the apostate enemy.

The People's Palace of Heavenly Delights was one of Pyongyang's premier restaurants. It was one of only three dining establishments in the city which had ready access to the food it sold at what, by North Korean standards, was priced outrageously high. A single meal at the People's Palace cost well beyond what an ordinary worker would earn in two months. The elite of every nation which enjoyed relations with the Democratic People's Republic of Korea met there periodically. The Foreign Press Club, to the extent there was such an organization functioning in Kim Jong-un's empire, regularly dined on the succulent splendors created there.

This evening promised to be an auspicious one. The two delegations who'd concluded their business had booked a private room off the main dining area, which had been specially cordoned off.

Wong Lee Yin had mercilessly driven his crew of master chefs and sous chefs since one this afternoon, preparing an awesome variety of delectables. Shortly before the first guest was to arrive, one of the sous chefs came up to Wong Yee Lin.

"Master," he said, producing an official-looking document with the seal of the Democratic People's Republic, "by order of our freedom-loving government, the plate covered with the silver dragon is to be set aside for the head of the Islamic State's delegation, Mister al-Taey. You will make certain that no one but the Mister al-Taey eats the food on that plate. Any food he does not eat, you will dispose of instantly. Do you understand?"

"Yes, of course."

An hourandahalf later, after consuming his entire meal, al-Taey rose to address the assembly. He spoke for close to twenty minutes before closing, "Gentlemen," he said, "In the next ten years, I believe the entire world will recognize the eternal brotherhood of the Democratic People's Republic and the Caliphate of the Islamic State, and will join us in leading the world to purity of thought and deed as together we eradicate the evil empire of the heathen, leading to a peaceful world, a world full of greater promise than ever."

The representative of the Caliphate had just started to call on a man in the back of the room, when suddenly he grabbed his stomach. Without another word, he collapsed. The coroner who performed the autopsy said it must have been a particularly virulent form of food poisoning. Although those who attended the dinner feared for their own lives during the next ten days, not one other guest experienced the slightest discomfort.

For the fifth straight day, Al-Raqqah, the Islamic State's Syrian capital, found itself under a double siege. First, of course, from the incessant summer heat. The thermometer read 110° Fahrenheit in the shade every day. Second, the clear, cloudless skies made daily bombing runs at any time of the day or night a very real threat. This morning, the normally quiescent wives and children of suicide bombers had chosen to stage a strike, which had turned into a riot. Fed up with the Islamic State's providing them with minimum levels of care and comfort when their husbands, brothers, fathers, and sons went out on *jihad* suicide missions, these women and children openly questioned what purpose, if any, was served by such folly.

# PART FOUR – CHAPTER 19

Abdul Rahman al-Afari, a former detainee at the U.S. military at Camp Bucca, Iraq, was charged with running a sponsorship program for the families of suicide bombers, assuring *jihadis* that their families would be cared for, should they agree to take on a suicide mission.

At this moment, his attention was riveted on an angry male voice which seemed to emanate from the middle of the crowd. "To hell with what the Caliphate is trying to do. Don't you see, they're all out for themselves? If you are all widowed, there are simply more females available for those cowards who *don't* go out on suicide missions. What does accepting their dirty money mean? Are we any less whores because our dead husbands will be watching from *alijann* while we're lying underneath those brutes who sent them out to die? We should find machine guns, walk into the Caliph's offices, and gun down every one of 'em. Blast 'em off the face of the earth!"

Shocked to hear such blasphemy, Abdul Rahman al-Afari was so intent on watching the reaction of the crowd to such unsanctioned remarks that he completely missed the tall man in a short-sleeve open-necked khaki outfit who took direct aim and dispatched him with a single bullet to the heart. When al-Afari's bodyguard hastened to where the shooter had been thirty seconds before, all he found in the dirt was a silver-colored golf ball.

The Islamic State is unlike any other terrorist group in the world. It has to keep hidden while also running a state. That has created a clandestine group of leaders anxious to protect themselves from rivals and airstrikes, but who must also engage in the mundane business of running a government. They not only order executions and devise military campaigns, but they also issue traffic tickets, regulate the price of food, and consider whether cigarettes and motorbike racing are acceptable to their brand of Islam. Who these men are remains mostly a mystery. But security intelligence agencies, mostly in the West, have tracked information from ISIS publications, from defectors, and from others to piece together the clearest possible picture of the top leaders of the Islamic State. Some patterns have emerged. Almost all of the Islamic State's most influential figures are Iraqi; many were once Saddam loyalists; several were detained by the U.S. military in Camp Bucca, Iraq.

Since 2010, the unquestioned leader of the Islamic State, the *primer inter pares*, and the self-designated Caliph, has been 45-year-old Abu bakr al-Baghdadi, who allegedly possesses a doctorate in Islamic law from Baghdad Islamic University, who served as an Imam in several prominent mosques across Iraq, and who was chosen by the Shura Council to lead the Islamic State of Iraq more than six years before.

In his undisclosed headquarters, which kept shifting almost daily in order to keep his whereabouts unknown to any but his closest associates, and to keep his head firmly attached to the rest of his body, al-Baghdadi had hastily convened a meeting of his closest associates, his designated successor and number two man, Abu Muslim al-Afari al-Turkmani, leader of the Provincial Council and Deputy Leader for Iraq; Abu Ali al-Anbari, leader of the Security and Intelligence Council and Deputy Leader for Syria; Abu Arkan al-Amiri, leader of the Shura Council, Omar al-Shishani, Chief of Staff; and Abu Yahya al-Iraqi, al-Baghdadi's personal bodyguard, who was never out of the Caliph's presence and who, unknown even to the man he was sworn to protect with his own life, was a spy for Anbari.

## PART FOUR – CHAPTER 19

Together the six of them represented the present, and, in the event anything happened to al-Baghdadi, the immediate future of Daesh, the Islamic State of Iraq and the Levant. The mood in the room was grim.

"Gentlemen," al-Baghdadi began. "I can understand one strange death within a two-week period. Maybe, and it's a long shot, two. Four is inconceivable. What makes it even more obvious are those golf balls found near the incidents."

"A plot, Caliph?" Anbari asked. He was the critical man in any investigation, the representative of Security and Intelligence.

"If I said yes, I'd be called paranoid. Not for the first time," al-Baghdadi said. "But I'm still alive. Just because you're paranoid does not mean they're *not* out to get you. Cautious suspicion is necessary if you want to stay alive."

The Security Chief was aware that despite the world viewing the boss man as a "wacko" or a "crazy," al-Baghdadi was no different from politicians the world over, from time out of mind. At bedrock, he was a cold, calculating pragmatist, who said whatever he had to say to stay in power, while hoping his electorate would forget whatever promises he had made when he was seeking public office.

"Ali, have you found anything from those of our sworn enemies who provide us information from time to time?" al-Turkmani asked.

"Nothing from the Syrian National Coalition, the SNC, the National Coalition for Syrian Revolutionary and Opposition Forces, the CCASG, or even the apostate Al-Nusra."

"Anything from al-Assad's people?"

"Unless they're keeping this very close to the chest, which is almost impossible, they believe it's us and the umbrella groups and no one else."

"Have there been any mysterious killings, infiltrations, or disappearances among the other groups?"

"Not to anyone's knowledge. We're the only apparent targets."

Al-Baghdadi pinched his beard between his thumb and forefinger."What kind of activities have there been on the ground?"

"Troubling," Anbari responded. "Historically we lose about a thousand soldiers a month. In the last three-and-a-half months we've lost almost eight thousand."

"More than double the average." This from al-Shishani. "I've heard reports that a much larger than usual number have suffered 'different' kinds of death."

"Face it, Shishani," the bodyguard said. "Whoever's doing these killings is taking a page out of our program. 'Different,' as in emasculations, stuffing testicles down a man's throat or up his …?"

"Enough," al-Baghdadi said. "Is there any particular sector where there are more killings than others?"

"No, Caliph," Anbari replied. "The deaths appear to be entirely random."

"Any unusual traffic in the neighborhood?"

"Our recruits continue at 7,500 or so each month. Most of 'em use Turkey, but the borders are quickly tightening up. They land at Istanbul, make it overland to Akçakale, then into Tell Abyad."

"That's not uncommon," al-Baghdadi said. "Have any of our people reported anything *unusual*? Abu, you were in military intelligence under Saddam. Obviously if no one in Iraq or Syria knows anything, whoever's polluting *Sharia* is coming from outside. If we've lost eight thousand, we're not talking a couple hundred guerillas. Let's assume ten thousand troops at a minimum. Air support?"

"There've been a few C5's, huge old cargo planes, showing up in airspace from Egypt to Iran. The Great Satan has running-dogs that would allow them to land anywhere, but they'd most likely restrict them to military bases, the American base at Incirlik, Selah Shalom in the Zionist fascist occupier of Palestine, Riyadh Air Force Base, Abu Suwayr Air Base in Egypt, and Muwaffak Salti Airbase in Jordan are the most likely places they'd land troops if the U.S. is behind this."

"As I'm sure they would be."

"Not necessarily," Turkmani replied. "To quote a cynical American statement, we're making enemies faster than we can kill them. I don't mean that in a bad way, My Caliph. Eventually the world will come to realize we're doing Allah's work for the greater good of the world."

"If we're still around," al-Baghdadi muttered under his breath. Out loud he said, "How many Americans are currently enlisted in our forces? I know you can't give me an exact figure, Anbari, but get as close as you can."

"Almost impossible to say, Caliph. The best guess I can give you is between ten and a hundred."

"Less Mohamad Jamal Khweis," Baghdadi said sardonically, mentioning the American whom Peshmerge forces had captured two months before. "Was he a fighter or a suicide jihadist?"

"Fighter."

"Of course. The Americans all want to come and fight for the cause and topple the Dictator. They just don't want to die doing it. Do we have any list of recent American arrivals?"

"Two Mexican Americans came in three months ago. A fellow who calls himself Chuey Garza. He pictures himself as a great hero but wouldn't take a risk if it meant he'd damage a fingernail. The second man who came across the border with Garza, Jorge Robles, seems smarter."

"How'd they enter Syria?" Baghdadi asked.

"A new driver, Ezeera al-Kayenne, who was recruited in Istanbul, was able to get them in through Akçakale. Kayenne has proved to be very adept at smuggling men and women through 'closed' borders."

"Is there reason to be suspicious of this very adept smuggler?"

"Of course, Caliph. Everyone's a potential enemy. We learned of him through our most successful recruiter in America, Imam Jarallah, who vouched for him."

"Interesting," the Caliph said, scratching his thick beard. "How do these Mexicans serve us?"

"Garza's a functionary in the tax collector's office. Robles is a traffic cop in Mosul."

The head of the Islamic State sighed. "It's the same in every society. The heroes die for the cause. The rank and file glorify these fighters and three days later the heroes are forgotten. The bureaucrats perpetuate themselves and live peacefully until they die in their beds at ninety. Which do you think we'll be, Abu?"

"Hard to say, Caliph."

"A typical bureaucratic answer, my friend. One thing's for certain, though. If we want to live longer than tomorrow, we'd best find out everything we can about this new threat. Garza and Robles are Americans. They can infiltrate the American air base in Turkey easier than we can. If we can somehow find this Ezeera al-Kayenne, so much the better."

# 20

---

"THANK you for meeting with me, Mister Kayenne." Al-Baghdadi looked over the "very adept driver," trying to take the measure of the man. Fifty, perhaps. Hard to tell, really. When a man got to be a certain age, the process of aging usually slowed for a decade, even two. Medium build, average height. A man one might easily forget five minutes after you'd met him. One who'd disappear into the background of a crowd, even if he were in plain sight.

"I trust you wanted me to come to Beirut for a reason, Mister al-Baghdadi." No "Caliph," no "Your Honor," no abject humility, and, most notably, not the slightest hint of fear. The man's Arabic was letter-perfect, accentless, with a dialect so pure it could have been native to anywhere in the region.

"You don't seem that impressed with me, Mister Kayenne."

"Nor do I seem particularly impressive to you," Kayenne responded

"You are not Muslim?"

"Perhaps, perhaps not. Is it that important?"

"Not really. You've been told why I requested this meeting. Do you mind if I ask your nationality?"

"Human."

Al-Baghdadi raised his eyebrows. "You are sophisticated and astute. I sense you're something more than a 'driver?'"

"Which of us is paying for the tea and baklava?" Kayenne asked, smiling to let the ISIS leader know that was not important.

"What information can you share with me?"

"You're aware that the C5s have been landing at Incirlik and elsewhere."

"How many?"

"Five flights a day. For awhile it was twice that."

"You seem well-versed in what is going on. Yet you drive for us?"

"I don't really have a dog in this hunt."

"Clever, Mister Kayenne. You know what we call dogs in this part of the world?"

"Supersized vermin. I find what is going on to be more a matter of interest than of side-taking. I have my own loyalties. That's as far as I'll go."

"Troops?"

"How many do you think, Caliph?"

"Fifteen thousand?" al-Baghdadi put out what, to him, was a high figure.

"Significantly more, Mister al-Baghdadi." The leader of the Islamic State paled for a brief moment, but said nothing. "More than enough to do the job."

"Is there a price on my head?"

"Could be."

# PART FOUR – CHAPTER 20

"You talk in riddles. Al-Kayenne is not your real name?"

"It's close enough for our purposes, Caliph Abu. Since you've been everything from a lawyer to a cleric to a soccer player to a courier for Al-Qaeda, you understand the game."

"What do you want from me?"

"I believe we want the same thing."

"Legitimacy?"

"It cuts both ways, Excellency." Kayenne put deliberate emphasis on the last word. The unspoken message was clear. *If you want to be treated like a state player instead of a rogue player, act like one. If you want to survive as a state, you have to be a member of the family of nations, not a tin-pot bully and dictator.*

"Is there some way I can contact you further if we need to talk?"

"You found me easily enough to set up this meeting."

"Do you mind if I ask …?"

"Yes, Mister al-Baghdadi, I do mind. I repeat, you found me easily enough to set up this meeting."

ॐ

"These people are very, very serious," al-Baghdadi reported back to his council. "He provided enough information to let me know the rules of the game have changed, but no more than that. They're using unmarked aircraft, they have no identifying uniforms, and we have no idea who their leaders are. Their strategy and tactics are a complete mystery. We have no idea how or where they'll strike next. Interesting, but unnerving to say the least."

As Caliph al-Baghdadi had pointed out, heroes die young and are quickly forgotten. Those who oil the wheels of the machinery of state seem to survive into decent age. Fares Reif al-Naima, whose *nom de guerre*, Abu Shema "Guardian of the Warehouses," was one of the latter. Al-Naima had fought against the Americans during the Iraq war, had been detained for awhile at Camp Bucca, and, although he joined the insurgency upon his release, he had had his bellyful of war. Now he served as Chief of Logistics and Supplies. Although nominally a member of the Islamic State's Military Council, his real job was to manage ISIS's weaponry and supplies and to coordinate the caliphate's mail system.

Even bureaucrats occasionally die of sudden illness or automobile accidents, or similar random events. It was therefore not necessarily surprising that Fares Reif al-Naima met his maker in a motor vehicle collision one night shortly after Caliph al-Baghdadi returned from his meeting in Lebanon with the man he knew only as Ezeera al-Kayenne.

What was unusual, however, was that the incident took place at nine in the evening on a Tuesday night when, so far as anyone knew, there was not a single other vehicle on the road and whoever had been driving the other car had simply disappeared, that no parts of the other vehicle were ever found, and that the floor inside the driver's side of the deceased's vehicle contained four pink golf balls.

## PART FOUR – CHAPTER 20

It was widely reported in the Western Media that Abu al Athir Amr al-Absi, the former ISIS governor of Aleppo province, a member of the Supreme Shura Council, and the Chairman of the Media Council, who was responsible for promoting and propagandizing the Islamic State, perished in an airstrike over the town of Maasa, near Syria's largest city, on March 3, 2016. The report was completely fabricated by al-Absi's propaganda machine at al-Baghdadi's direction.

Al-Absi, better known as Abu al-Atheer, exemplified several key dynamics at work in Syria. He had been among the jihadi-Salafists released by Bashar al-Assad's regime at the beginning of Syria's uprising in an attempt to make self-fulfilling the regime's claim that the opposition were terrorists. He was also instrumental in making Syria so dangerous for journalists that it allowed Assad and the Islamic State to shape the coverage as if Syria was a tennis match between them. Atheer was a longstanding ultra-extremist, who shaped and defined the State's infiltration and expansion in Syria, particularly by bringing in foreigners, the most ideologically driven ISIS members.

A week after Fares Reif al-Naima's death, while the media and propaganda director was on holiday on the Mediterranean, just north of the Lebanese frontier, an elderly gentleman, who vaguely reminded al-Absi of his late father's closest friend, albeit now much older, approached the younger man.

"Good morning, my younger Brother!" The older man stood in the early morning sun and waved to the Shura member. "How are you this morning?"

Al-Absi's face broke out into a broad grin. "Are you truly Nasr al-Abdullah?"

"I am indeed. You've grown quite tall and that thick beard becomes you, Boy. I remember that sweet smile from years ago. I am so pleased to see my old friend's son has risen so far in the hierarchy. I understand you're calling yourself al-Atheer these days."

The ISIS minister blushed with pleasure.

"You are well then, Youngster?"

"Praise Allah, I am."

"I'm delighted." The old man produced a small plastic bag. "I brought you a present from my garden."

As al-Absi glanced inside the bag, he looked ecstatic. "My God, you remembered. This is the rarest treat of all. I have loved your mangoes since I was five years old!" He opened the bag wider and looked down. "Only one this time?"

"Only one," al-Abdullah said. "The last of the year's crop. But it is ripe and ready to eat."

"Then we must share it," al-Absi responded.

"No, al-Atheer. I have enjoyed them all season. This one's my special gift to you. I noticed you were on your way to the seashore. Enjoy this gift from the heart, my young friend."

Ten minutes later, as he walked onto the sandy beach, al-Absi reached into the bag, and in great anticipation, pulled out the small, orangecolored ovoid. A moment later, his remains were splattered across the sand as the grenade exploded.

When the police investigators surveyed the grisly scene that confronted them, they found three amethyst-colored golf balls.

## PART FOUR – CHAPTER 20

Another plenary meeting, this time at the Aegean beachside resort at Kuşadası, Turkey.

"Six down. We've struck down one of the Shura council," Tommy Aiello crowed. His subordinate generals spontaneously applauded. "Ezra," he said, deferring to his Israeli comrade in arms, "I understand their highest leader reached out to you and you met with him in Beirut three weeks ago."

"Correct," Caen replied. "He knew me only as a driver who delivered ISIS recruits into Akçakale, but it quickly became obvious he wanted information about aircraft landings, troop deployment, and numbers. My responses were deliberately vague, but I conveyed the message that there were more than enough to take care of the job. I also convinced him I didn't have a horse in this race and I would not be pulled into further conversation."

"Did you read anything else into what he said?" O'Brien asked.

"I did," Caen responded. "Whether it's our doing or not, al-Baghdadi came right out and said his Islamic State was looking for legitimacy."

"How did you answer him?" General Gigante asked.

"By addressing him with the single word, 'Excellency,' not 'Caliph' or 'Leader' or any religious honorific. I implied, and this man is by no means stupid, that if the Islamic State wanted to be treated like a state player instead of a rogue, it must act like a state player. If the Islamic State wanted to survive, it would have to be a member of the family of nations, not a murderer-pariah."

"You think we're having an effect?" Tommy asked.

"I *know* we're having an effect," Ezra replied. "But now is not the time to ease up on these folks. Al-Baghdadi may be the present Caliph, but the Shura can vote him out of office. Anywhere there's power to be had, there will be dissenting voices ready to seize that power the moment they sense any lack of resolve."

"Gentlemen," the Field Marshal said, "While I salute your strategy and tactics, may I suggest a most unladylike, and certainly a most abhorrent, *un*-nunlike event?..."

Even the unflappable counterterrorists, Ezra Caen and Manucher Tabrizi, were astonished by Sister Maureen's suggestion.

"Sister," Tommy Aiello said, not without a sense of awe, "Did anyone ever suggest you'd have been the most feared and powerful *Donna* ... uh, *Don* ... of all?"

༺༻

"What foolish insane sacrilege is this?" al-Baghdadi practically screamed at his Shura Council. "How in Merciful Allah's name did they manage to find us? How could they have had the ... the *balls* ... to suggest such an outrage?"

The normally calm, measured ISIS leader was nearly apoplectic with rage.

Sitting on a table in front of him was an engraved invitation in fluent Arabic, on heavy, cream-colored vellum paper. There were four engraved, gold-colored golf balls, one in each corner of the message, which read,

## PART FOUR – CHAPTER 20

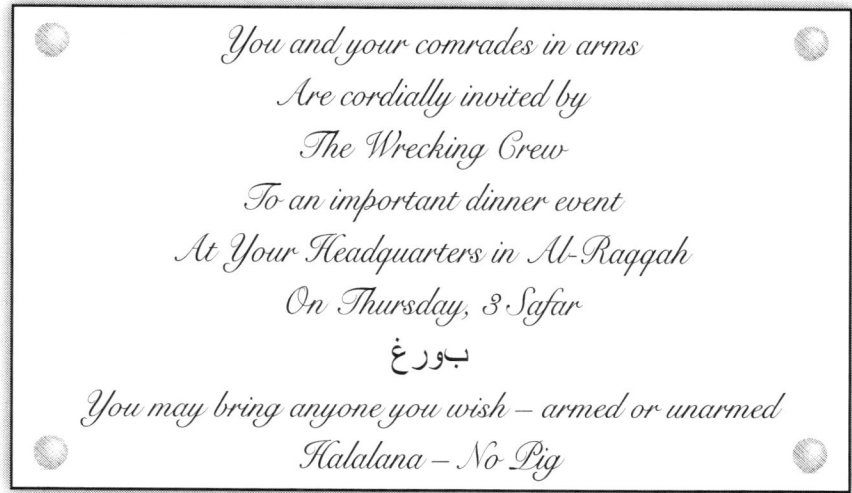

There was no other writing.

Shortly after 1:30 a.m. on November 3, the twenty night shift guards in the Islamic State's Headquarters Building were suddenly, silently overpowered, bound, gagged, and driven fifty miles beyond the city limits, where they were unceremoniously dumped in the middle of the desert. They were replaced by a hooded phalanx dressed in "Afghani robes," who took up guard stations; plus a group of sixteen others, fifteen of whom walked with a decidedly stiff, shuffling gait. The sixteenth, smaller than the others, spoke softly in a higher register. Within the next hour, fifty "caterers" silently carried the makings of a feast into a large vault in the basement of the building. After this had been done, the caterers and sixteen "replacement" security guards secreted themselves in abandoned library facilities in a far end of the basement, while the remaining twenty remained on duty in the front.

In the morning, the visible basement guards were advised that while they were free to sleep during the day, no one was to leave the building for the next twenty-four hours. At noon that day, under the personal supervision of Abu Ali al-Anbari, Leader of the Security and Intelligence Council and Abu Yahya al-Iraqi, al-Baghdadi's personal bodyguard, the security contingent in the building and surrounding the outside of the Headquarters, was increased by a hundred. Anyone attempting to enter this impregnable fortress would clearly do so at the risk of his own life.

As the afternoon wore on, the anxiety level in the ISIS Headquarters Building increased. Caliph al-Baghdadi had chosen to absent himself in the highly unlikely event anyone breached the security arrangements. Telephone calls were unanswered, which was to have a profound effect since at least three of them came from outlying areas to which the original security guards from the night before had been driven.

The sun set at 4:41 that afternoon. Between five and five-thirty, two of the three main religious leaders, Turki al-Binali, who'd been expelled from the Emirates for his "corrupt beliefs," and Osman al-Nazeh al-Asiri, who had helped prevent defections from the Islamic State, as well as Abu Arkan al-Amiri, leader of the Shura Council, Omar al-Shishani, the Georgia-born Chief of Staff, Abu Ayman al-Iraqi, a member of the Shura Council, and Abu Muhammad al-Adnani, council spokesman appeared with their bodyguards. Shortly thereafter, they were joined by members of the Provincial Council, the Military Council, the Security and Intelligence Council, the Religious Affairs Council, the Finance Council, and the Media Council. Each of these stalwarts was also accompanied by his bodyguard. Two of the top three men in the leadership, Caliph al-Baghdadi, and Abu Muslim al Afari al-Turkmani, Leader, Provincial Council, Deputy for Iraq, and al-Baghdadi's heir presumptive, had conspicuously absented themselves. The number three man in the Islamic State, Abu Ali al-Anbari, Leader of the Security and Intelligence Council and Deputy leader for Syria, entered the room.

At precisely 6:15 p.m., twenty security guards, machine guns at the ready, entered the banquet room. They were followed by fifty caterers bearing trays of fresh vegetables, fruits, sweetmeats, rice, tabouleh, tahini, and assorted sauces. Half the caterers then remained in the room, unholstering weapons of their own. The other twenty-five went back to the basement. They returned shortly, bearing the meat course. As the attendees gazed first in rapt anticipation and then in horror, they beheld the evenings *pieces de resistance*: a properly stuffed, roasted pair of whole sheep, a ram and a ewe, two of what appeared to be roasted human beings, males, but without the genitalia and cleansed of the internal organs, and, surrounding the four bodies, various parts of the necks, legs, and organ meats, and a selection of testicles, which, it was very obvious, did not come from the sheep. Finally, there were at least two hundred golf balls of different colors spread over the plates.

While the guests were gasping and some had turned a sickly pallor, fifteen elderly men entered in large hall wearing military outfits with crossed bandoliers and machine guns. The final person to enter was a small woman dressed in Roman Catholic nun's habit.

The ISIS bodyguards started to raise their own arms, but a glare from the tallest of the old men followed by a single wagging finger raised in a universal warning caused them to stand down.

"Gentlemen," Tommy said in halting, simple Arabic, "my name is Tomaso Giovanni Aiello. This dinner is sponsored by the Vatican State. Our leader, the Reverend Sister Maureen

Cerone Richards, will now lead us in prayer, *and you had better pray*."

Sister Maureen stepped to a nearby raised podium, gave a brief prayer exhorting love and brotherhood throughout the world, and sat down.

Tiny General Gigante asked in Arabic if there was anyone in the room who spoke English. When someone gingerly raised his hand, Gigante signaled him to move to the front of the room, where Tommy "Legs" Aiello had mounted the dais again. This time he spoke in English while the English-speaking member of the Islamic State translated.

"Men of the Islamic State, we are delighted you chose to join us this evening. I'm sure many of you are wondering how in Allah's name, or how in Hell, we got here. That is really of not your concern. The fact is we *are* here and that shows we are capable of showing up *anywhere* in the Islamic State at any time. We don't depend on anyone to tell us *when* we can appear or *where* we can appear, or even *how* we can appear. The number of men in *The Wrecking Crew* need not affect you. Let's simply say we have enough to get the job done, and make no mistake, we *will* get the job done.

"We could shoot and kill everyone in this room. We have the firepower to do it. We could cut off the heads or the hands of our victims, just as you have done. We can rid ourselves of your leadership, as we have already proved six times. We could shoot you in the knees or elbows, so you would never walk without pain again and you could never reach for bread again.

"But we choose to do none of those things. As you look around at our small number, each of you can see with your own eyes that none of us is a young man. I can assure you there is not one of us who has not been responsible for killing or crippling at least a hundred men, in some cases as many as seven times that number. Each of us has chosen this as his profession.

"I'm told the rams' testicles are a great delicacy in this part of the world. What you see before you are testicles, but they are not rams' testicles. This is your feast, not ours. You are our guests. We will leave the room to go back to where we came from in a few moments. You will not harm a hair on our heads and we will not harm a hair on your heads. Tomorrow each of us will return to our lives to do what we have to do, we among our own, you among your own. So, gentlemen, my speech is concluded. You may dine *on your own*."

With that, the Field Marshal, the Generalissimo, the fourteen subordinate generals, and the rest of the Wrecking Crew's contingent smartly left the room.

Not one shot was fired on either side.

# 21

"**Chuey,** do you get the feeling we may have been dissed?"

"Yeah. We were told we were gonna help deliver humanitarian goods to people who were fighting a bad dictator. What's up with that? I'm moving papers from one side to the other in an office that's trying to force people who can't afford to buy shit to pay half of whatever they've got in taxes that go to support weapons and suicide fighters. This is bullshit!"

"It's no better for me, *Essay*," Jorge Robles responded. "I'm directing traffic in Mule's Ass, Iraq. I see fifteen cars a day. Directing traffic means they wait an hour at a time while the head honcho of a military group that's getting the shit kicked out of them drives his big fuckin' Humvee in front of a few old, beaten-up trucks."

"Jorge, do you ever get the feeling we're working for …" Garza turned his head, looked around to make sure no one was watching, and lowered his voice to just above a whisper, "the bad guys?"

"Uh-huh. They look like KKKs. You never see the whole face."

"Did you ever think to bounce?" Chuey asked. Jorge noticed his hand was shaking with a nervous tremor.

"Shhh, Chuey. The walls have ears. Later."

"When? Where?"

"Sundown. *Ma'an Sharie* at the far end of the city. There's a Kurdish lokanta there."

※

Their conversation was conducted quietly, completely in Oaxacan dialect.

"I've been a loud-mouthed *gilipollas* for as long as I can remember. I was always *el cabrón*. After I got out of juvie I thought maybe if I did some good for someone far away from Salinas, I could get a new start in a place where no one knew me."

"Seems like a grown-up thing to do," Jorge said.

"Yeah, but then I got into a knife fight with you ... I'm really sorry, *Essay*, I was pushed into it ... no, Jorge, that's bullshit, too. I thought maybe if I could stand up just once ..."

"I'm not blaming you, Chuey. It takes two to tango."

"Maybe. But I got us both kicked off the bus. One thing led to another and here we are on the wrong side ..." Robles noticed that his companion was choking back tears. "Jorge, I am scared shitless. These people really are the bad guys and they play for keeps. H-h-h-have you seen the videos they're sending out?"

"Uh-huh."

"For the past two weeks my bossman has been throwing all kinds of hints at me. 'You know, you're young and strong. You should really be fighting on the front lines. Seems you've been ducking the *real* service to the Cause…'"

"Scary shit, Chuey."

"Worse than that, Jorge. He doesn't miss a chance to let me know the Movement, that's what they call it, doesn't like to feed someone who's not carrying his weight. He even talked about suicide bombers. Shit, if there was only some way I could get outta' this fucking place. But they've got the borders sealed up tighter than …"

"Is there anyone you can talk to, Chuey?"

"Other than you, no."

"I wonder whatever happened to those guys on the bus?"

"You really don't know?"

"Uh-uh."

"They're over here, only they're on the *other* side."

"How do you know that?"

"Sometimes when I go out to the camps to deliver money to the captain, I hear things. A couple of guys talking quietly … A few of them speak some English. I heard words like *muchacho, hombre, cojones,* the kind of words they've never heard in this part of the world. What's more, they seemed more scared of the *other* guys than I'm scared of them."

"So it's true what the recruiters said."

"Yeah, Jorge. As much as we don't know how the hell we got roped in, we're with what America calls ISIS."

"No shit, *Essay*. D'you think there's any way we could contact the good guys?"

## PART FOUR – CHAPTER 21

"I wish. That's been why 'our' forces are so frightened of them. They show up when nobody expects it, where nobody expects them to be."

"I've heard rumors of guys that every time they kill somebody or cut 'em up they leave a golf ball in the area."

"That's them, all right. But exactly how the hell do we try to get in touch with 'em? Put an ad in the ISIS paper? Good way to get your head chopped off in a hurry."

"How far to the nearest border, amigo?"

"We're not that far from Turkey. There's a shitload of refugees crossing into that country every day and every night. If only we could fit in with them without being watched."

⁂

Alas, as that moment, unknown to the two Hispanics, they were being watched by four of the most militant jihadis, men who had been specially selected to infiltrate pockets of resistance to the Islamic State's iron-fisted rule. Neither Chuey Garza nor Jorge Robles paid any attention to the men as, one by one, they left the restaurant.

At ten that night, Jorge and Chuey departed the lokanta. Jorge was the first to feel the knife softly pushed against his spine. Chuey was grabbed around the neck. "Keep walking, gentlemen," a surly voice commanded in English. "If you want to keep your heads attached to your shoulders for a few more minutes, you will not look back, you will not ask questions, and you will walk quietly with us. We're all friends, right?" he continued, clapping Jorge comradely on the shoulders.

"We're about to have a little lesson in *Sharia*, and what it means when you disobey Allah's law," a second voice snarled. "So we don't need to speak until we get where we're going."

With the four men at their back, Garza and Robles, the former now reduced to trembling, got to the end of the street before the assailants quickly grabbed their arms in a hammerlock and frog-marched them beyond the town limits.

There were no lights except for stars and the slightest sliver of crescent moon. Their terror escalated as they saw a group of ten men, bound, gagged, and kneeling pitifully on the ground. Two men were tying blindfolds around the heads of the prisoners.

"All right, infidels," the second voice addressed the Mexicans, "there is nothing more sinful in *Sharia* law than coming to the true faith with fraud and cowardice in your hearts. But Allah is all-merciful. In his honor, we will give you your choice. You choose your own fate. Do you wish to lose your right hand, your ears, your tongue, or your head. You have thirty seconds to decide."

Just as the two of them and the other prisoners had sobbed, prayed, and resigned themselves to their horrible fate, Chuey heard another sound, one that was absolutely impossible to conceive in the barren outskirts where they were about to take their last breaths: the distant thrum of a bowstring and the whir of flying arrows as they hurtled into the midst of the ISIS death team.

Chuey was beyond astonished to hear a rapidly repeated thrum-thrum-thrum and whir-whir-whir. It must have been an entire army sent to save them. It seemed to take only a few seconds, but in those seconds ten men, two-thirds of the ISIS death squad – lay dead, dying, or desperately mutilated.

## PART FOUR – CHAPTER 21

Those who remained alive raced back toward the city. Not quickly enough. Jorge saw three men at the top of a small rise, who, with incredible the speed and agility, were whipping other arrows from their quivers, knocking them to their bows, and shooting them so fast that their right arms were almost a blur, while their left hands, holding the bow grips, stayed as steady as statues. Within a few more moments, there were five more bodies writhing or still on the ground.

The prisoners' bodies were massive lumps of tension, their spirits had nearly been destroyed. Not long before, Chuey and Jorge had prayed for a swift end to their suffering. Neither of them knew what to think, what to believe, or even what to hope for. Had Mother Church or Father God truly sent three avenging angels or were the men coming down the hill simply other, larger captors, coming to seize the prey earlier taken by the ISIS killers?

The man who seemed to be the leader of the trio approached Chuey. "*Buenos noches, Señor Garza.* If you hadn't gotten into a stupid knife fight on the bus back in Southern California you might have been on the hill with us, shooting the bad guys. No hard feelings, *Muchacho*. The past is the past."

"You …? I … I know you …"

"Sixth grade back on Alisal. Acosta Plaza …."

He held out his hand. In his befuddled state, all Chuey Garza could do was grab it, cry all the harder, and get down on his knees, blubbering his eternal thanks.

"P – p – p …?"

"*Si, Amigos.* Pedro Sanchez, Miguel Hernandez, and Rodrigo Resendiz. Just three guys from the Wrecking Crew out for a late night stroll. Given the circumstances, it might not be a good idea to go back to your friends. You might want to stay with us for awhile. But first," he said, grabbing a golf ball out of each pocket, "it would be bad manners if we didn't leave our calling cards."

"Very ballsy, Mister Sanchez," Tommy said. He'd heard of Pedro's heroism of two nights before. Prior to that, the reports about the young Hispanic from Salinas had been uniformly favorable. "Do you have any suggestions as to what we should do with the two men whose lives you saved?"

"I do, General Aiello," Pedro responded calmly and confidently. "I knew Chuey Garza back in the sixth grade. He was a little sucker then and he didn't get much better as he grew up. But then again, neither did I. We both came from nothing and we were headed for nothing. I don't know how the knife fight started, since I was half asleep, but where else was he going to go after he got kicked off the bus? I got a second chance and I've got a whole lot to be thankful for. Is Chuey a bad kid? Maybe, maybe not. But should he get a chance to prove himself? I think so. The other fellow, Jorge Robles? I never knew him, but from everything I've seen and heard, he was simply a quiet guy who got pulled along for the ride."

"For a twenty-year-old, you're pretty damn wise, Sanchez. Should we send 'em back home?"

"General Aiello, those guys had the life scared out of them. Now they're in between hell and hell. Send 'em back, it's a one way ticket back to the *barrio*. Give 'em a chance to redeem themselves and who knows? They've been with the Islamic State for three months. That's not to say they've learned everything they need to know or even very much of what they need to know. But they know a lot more about the organization than we do. They believe they owe us their lives. Maybe they're right. Why don't we simply keep 'em in Iraq or Syria for a little while and use whatever knowledge they have to help *our* cause? Maybe even let them earn back what the recruiter promised in Salinas."

Tommy Aiello thought long and hard for a few moments. Then he looked at Pedro and said, "Mister Sanchez, if you could spare me for a few minutes, I'd like to make a telephone call."

While Tomaso Aiello was gone, Pedro busied himself in the outer office, reading a two-week-old copy of *Time* magazine which the Generalissimo had left on table adjacent to the sofa. When he got halfway through the magazine, he glanced at his watch. Twelve minutes. No big deal. The door to General Aiello's inner office opened and the eighty-two-year-old *Don* invited Pedro Sanchez to come in.

"I'll get straight to the point, Pedro ... may I call you that?"

"Of course, General."

"Tommy."

"Tommy?"

"Uh-huh. But only when we're alone because if you call me Tommy in public I'll have your tit in a wringer so fast you won't know what hit you. I just got off the phone with Sister Maureen."

"The big boss?"

"Yeah, she of the gold golf balls."

"I'm sorry. I should have left earlier."

"No you shouldn't have. We talked about you."

"Something I've done wrong, Sir?"

"Tommy."

"Tommy."

"Yeah, I guess you might say that. You're being relieved of combat duty, effective this moment."

"May I ask why, Sir?"

"You may indeed. I've been looking for a personal *aide de camp* for the last several weeks. I've found the guy I need. It's you, Pedro. From now on, you are *Captain* Pedro Sanchez. Not that it would make that much difference, since you've earned your four year college program and the government job, but your pay is changing. Effective tomorrow morning you'll be earning five thousand a month instead of twenty-five hundred."

Pedro, who'd always fancied himself nothing more than a soldier in the field trying to do the best he could, found himself speechless. The best he could muster was a simple, quiet, "Thank you, Sir."

"Oh, and there's one more thing, Captain Sanchez … While I was talking with Sister Maureen she told me that earlier this morning your *novia*, Angelina Morales, gave birth to a seven pound, three ounce daughter. Mother and baby doing fine. And you can FaceTime with her from my office if you want privacy."

# Part Five

# STING

# 22

"WE'RE beating 'em to shreds on the ground," Sister Maureen reported. "Fallujah's firmly back in Iraqi government hands. The Al-Raqqah stronghold is shaky. For the first time there are more deserters than recruits, but it won't stay that way for long."

"What is it they always say? When there's a 'but' in the sentence, you ignore everything that went before? We've weathered a shipload of political heat during the past few months. The shooter in Orlando, Trump with his, 'See, I told you this would happen.' The NRA and the control lobby saying, 'See, I told you this would happen.' All because one loose nut happened to say, 'I was inspired by ISIS.' He could have just as easily said Al-Qaeda, 'cause they're still in business. Even if the two of them don't even speak with one another, the great Middle America lumps them and the Taliban and everyone else who happens to hate the West into the same basket."

"It sure seems that way, Jim. Unlike most government enterprises, we're coming in way under budget," the Field Marshal said.

"So I've noticed," the FBI director said. "As, by the way, has Congress. How much longer do you think the operation will take?"

# PART FIVE – CHAPTER 22

"It'll never be over, Jim. You know that and I know that. We'll still be on the ground here awhile."

"Define 'awhile.'"

"'til we're done. That's not the reason I'm calling. I've got another request."

"Request or favor?"

"Both. I think you'll find it's more of a favor to the good guys than to me. Another crackpot idea, but if it works we can use it as a model for how we treat *all* the bad guys in the future."

"I sense another summit meeting?"

"A mini summit. You, Dennis, Ezra, Tommy, Manucher and me."

"Where and when?"

"As soon as possible. You name the place. And Jim?"

"Yes, Sister?"

"Since you're used to traveling around the world at a moment's notice, try to remember it's been a long, *hot* summer here."

※

When it was founded in 1830 as *Akmoly*, which means "white grave," *Astana* served as a defensive fortification for the Siberian Cossacks. In 1961 the city was renamed *Tselinograd*. In 1992, it went back to the name *Akmola*. In December 1997, it replaced Almaty as the capital of Kazakhstan. Five months later, it was renamed Astana. Like Brasilia, Canberra, and Washington, D.C., Astana is a planned city. As the seat of the

Kazakhstani government, it's the site of the Parliament House, the Supreme Court, the Presidential Palace and a number of futuristic buildings, hotels, and skyscrapers.

Despite its lovely, sonorous name, Astana is not the most hospitable place in the world. Located in central Kazakhstan on the Ishim River in a flat, semiarid steppe region, it's the second coldest capital city in the world after Ulaanbaatar, Mongolia. Summers are warm, with occasional brief rain showers. Winters are long, very cold, and dry. The lowest air temperature ever recorded in there was −60 °F. The city's river is usually frozen over between the second week of November and the beginning of April. Astana has a well-deserved reputation among Kazakhs for its frequent high winds. Still, it *is* the capital. That much, but not much more, can be said for it.

As Sister Maureen stepped off Air Astana Flight KC918 at 6:45 in the morning, the temperature was 5° Fahrenheit, fifty degrees colder than when she had boarded the Airbus 320 at Atatürk International five hours before. Fortunately, Astana Airport was heated to a comfortable seventy-two degrees and her 25-minute van ride to the Hilton Garden Inn started inside the airport building and dropped her off less than ten feet from the hotel entrance. The meeting had been scheduled for early afternoon. Since she'd slept well on the flight from Istanbul, she needed only a hot bath and three more hours of sleep to arrive at the meeting refreshed and ready to explain the plan she and her generals had been working on for the past week.

At noon, she descended to the lunch buffet, where Ezra Caen, Tommy Aiello, and Manucher Tabrizi, who'd flown in the day before, awaited her.

"Some change of climate you ordered, Sister," Tabrizi said sardonically. "As I recall, last year about this time we met in a place a bit more conducive to my tastes."

## PART FIVE – CHAPTER 22

"As if a day or two in refreshing Astana will freeze your poor little candy-arse off, Persian." This from Ezra.

"Generalissimo" Aiello, who felt stiff because of the cold, complained, "Is there any reason this meeting couldn't have been set up via a conference call? Much cheaper."

"Security," Maureen said simply. She glanced at her watch. "Eat up, guys. They should be here in ten minutes. How's Pedro working out, Tommy?"

"Great," the retired *Capo* said. "Bright, loyal as a dog, and creative. I wonder whether I should bring him into this when we get approval."

"When?" Ezra asked. "After what we've saved them so far, and given the magnitude of what could happen if this test works out, I'd think the entire Western world would be standing in line to fund this. Oh, hi, Jim, Dennis," he greeted the two FBI representatives. "Where are we supposed to meet?"

"Private room adjacent to mine," the Director said. "It's been thoroughly combed for bugs, and …"

"Isn't that crap a bit old-fashioned?" the Iranian counterterrorist asked. "Nowadays everyone simply assumes *somebody* somewhere is listening or looking or grabbing something out of the air."

"Hence Astana, Kazakhstan," O'Brien said. "A million miles from nowhere that anyone would care to go."

"Yeah, like Iran and Syria," Tommy added.

The room could have been a small conference room anywhere in the world: a large, oval wooden table, eight comfortable plush office chairs, a sideboard with a selection of teas, platters of cookies, and a coffee maker. A yellow legal pad, a selection of pens, and individual interconnected personal computers situated in front of each chair.

"First thing, let's unplug the computers," The FBI Director said. "The most obvious means to intercept anything we say or write." One or two nods and each attendee unplugged his or her unit. "All right, Sister, your meeting, your agenda," he continued.

"Thank you Jim, gentlemen. A couple months ago we held a meeting in Istanbul. All of our guys concluded that while we could beat up the ISIS forces on the ground by any number of tricks and strategies, we'd never eradicate every last one of them. People die. Ideas live on.

"So we started thinking, 'What's the most serious long-term threat from the Islamic Republic or any other extremist group?' The answer was right under our noses: Social Networks. They're all over the world and they've been ISIS's major recruiting tool. We're not just talking Facebook and Twitter. They're the largest in the world, but they're not the only ones."

"According to our intelligence, more than one billion people, one out of every six in the world, regularly tune in to Facebook," O'Brien said. "Whenever there's an ISIS-crisis anywhere, San Bernardino, Orlando, Paris, or whenever anyone wants to sell anything from a Presidential candidate to a tube of marijuana-flavored toothpaste, you'd better believe Twitter will be there."

Sister Maureen went over to the sideboard, selected a packet of Moroccan mint tea, and gently poured boiling water from the adjacent pot into a china cup.

"That's two," she said casually. "Name some more," she addressed her confreres.

A few answers came forth: Instagram, Pinterest, LinkedIn, followed by silence. Ezra Caen broke that silence: "WeChat," he said. "Six hundred fifty-million and growing every day. Nearly three quarters of a billion people and they don't just exchange pictures of what they had for lunch. If you're anywhere within half a world of China, you'd know that Facebook is a WeChat wannabe. WeChat is where you go to pay bills, hail rides, play casual games, browse news, send friends money … you name it. It's got millions of 'official accounts' on the platform which act as mini apps within the app, enabling users to interact with brands, services, even celebrities. I'm sure your esteemed FBI Director knows all about it, but how many of the rest of you are familiar with it?"

No one raised a hand.

"Then you've got WhatsApp," Ezra continued. "Facebook paid nineteen *billion* with a 'b,' dollars to buy that one. It's used by over 900 million people around the world. Thirty billion messages have been sent through its servers. Its popularity took off because it uses an internet connection to send messages instead of traditional cellular networks, so messages don't count against the allotment from your wireless carrier. Another reason WhatsApp spread quickly around the world is that it populates your 'friends' list with phone numbers already on your phone. You can find a contact that works without having to look up a separate email address or username."

"Interesting," The FBI Director murmured with what everyone around the table knew was much more than a little interest.

"But not unknown," Ezra concluded. "You can Google 'Social Media networks' or 'App download networks' and get that information almost instantly."

Within ten minutes, the participants, each using their own OS SmartPhones, their Android phones, or their small wifi-enabled personal computers came up with a list of sixteen additional treasure troves of human communication:

**Messenger**
**Tweetie**
**Snapchat**
**Path**
**Timehop**
**GroupMe**
**Periscope**
**Meerkat**
**Yo**
**Highlight**
**FireChat**
**Tinder**
**YikYak**
**Vine**
**Kik**
**Tumblr**

"That may not cover every potential recruit in the world, but it's a huge chunk of them," Sister Maureen said. "We can find more as we go along, but what we need is a device which can hack into and replace as many recruiting efforts as we can find. Once we do that, we've got to be ready to move and adapt instantly."

"Sort of like the '50s and '60s," Tommy remarked. "When shortwave stations like Radio Moscow jammed other stations like Voice of America, and those stations that had been jammed immediately found a new frequency until it got jammed again."

"Exactly, Tommy. To do that today, we need one humongously big machine."

## PART FIVE – CHAPTER 22

"Like the Cray Titan," The FBI Director remarked.

At the questioning looks from the others, the FBI Director briefly explained the workings of the world's third most powerful computer, the Cray Titan, which was able to perform more than one thousand *trillion* operations per second, a speed of 17.59 petaflops. "Although the Titan is much slower than the two Chinese supercomputers, the Sunway TaihuLight which, at 93 petaflops, recently replaced the Tianhe-2, which functions at a speed of 34 petaflops, it's currently the best we've got," he said, grinning. "I think it'll be more than sufficient to do the job."

It soon became apparent that the sheer audacity of what Ezra, Manucher, Sister Maureen, and Tommy Aiello proposed was so astonishing in its outrageous, insanely elegant *simplicity* that the FBI guys quickly became addicted to the idea.

"If this works ..." The FBI Director said, "and I can't see how it *can't* work, it could become the model to use against every terrorist organization, every radicalized movement, every crackpot scheme to lure in gullible, go-for-broke recruits. It doesn't matter if it's ISIS, Al-Qaeda, the Taliban, or some weirdo-wacko offshoot organization that hasn't even been invented yet. Of course, it would cost quite a bit of money, but then again, which civilized state player can you think of who *wouldn't* want to jump on board?"

# 23

IN March 1981, a country-western group, The Oak Ridge Boys, recorded a song written fifteen years before by Bakersfield-raised songwriter Dallas Frazier. The song, *Elvira*, raced up both the country and pop charts. Six months later, it had sold two million copies. The group that had originated in Knoxville, Tennessee in the 1940s, adopted the name "The Oak Ridge Boys" because they'd been hired almost every weekend to perform for staff members and families stationed during World War II at the nuclear research plant in Oak Ridge, Tennessee, thirty miles away. By 1981, most young Americans who hummed and sang *Elvira* had hardly even heard of Oak Ridge, let alone knew anything about the place. But things had been different, way different, during the Second World War.

Oak Ridge, established in 1942 as a production site for the Manhattan Project, developed the atomic bomb. Back then, it was known as *the Atomic City*, *the Secret City*, *the Ridge*, or *the City Behind the Fence*.

Today, the United States Department of Energy runs Oak Ridge National Laboratory, a nuclear high-tech research establishment at the site, and performs national security work.

## PART FIVE – CHAPTER 23

Until it was surpassed in 2013 by China's Tianhe-2, the Cray Titan at Oak Ridge was the world's fastest and most powerful supercomputer. As of September 2016 it's still number three, no mean feat.

Sister Maureen, Ezra, and Tommy Aiello had been charged with telling the operative who'd been assigned to them, what they wanted. None of them had any objections when Aiello suggested his aide-de-camp, Pedro Sanchez, join them, "to bring someone the youngsters on campus can identify with."

As they entered the inner sanctum of the laboratory housing the Cray, they were met by a tall, casually-dressed man in his late thirties with thinning hair and a thick, bushy red beard, who held out his hand as if he'd known each of them for years.

"Hi, I'm JaysonElliott," he said. "JaysonElliott, one word, no hyphen, and yes, Jayson is my first name and Elliott's my last name. I've been called JaysonElliott for so long the name sorta' just stuck." The man exuded warmth. Although he was not particularly handsome in the classic sense, his ready smile and eager-to-help-in-any-way-I-can attitude was magnetic.

"The Feds gave me an outline of what it is you're looking for. I wish I'd have come up with the idea. I about peed my pants laughing the first time I'd heard of it. Then I started doing a preliminary workup and the idea got better and better."

"We'd hoped you'd feel that way about it Jayson … er … JaysonElliott," Sister Maureen said.

"Smart idea to hack into the number of networks you're thinking about, even though most of ISIS's business these days seems to be conducted on Twitter," the computer expert said. "What have you guys, pardon me, Sister, you folks …?"

"'Guys' is perfectly okay," Maureen rejoined.

"What have you done about producing content?"

"Giacomo Dragna, our guy from L.A.'s in charge of the skin," Tommy said. At questioning looks from the others, he explained, "Porno. All kinds, gonzo, straight, Lesbian, gay, bi, transgender …"

"Transgender?" Pedro exclaimed, shocked.

"Yeah, that plays well nowadays. Whips, chains, sado-masochistic stuff. All hard core and good lookers. Asian, Black, Native American, you name it."

"How did Dragna do that?" Ezra asked. Clearly he was looking at these disclosures as knowledge to be used, not games to titillate or horrify.

"The family's got 'interests' in all fifty the major Canoga Park producers, Greg Dunn at Anabolic, Dion Giarrusso at Combat Zone, John Stagliano at Elegant Angel, Janet Romano at Extreme…"

"A *female*?" Pedro asked. He was clearly getting the type of education one didn't get at Alisal High School.

"Pedro," Tommy said patiently, "more than half the owners and directors in the business have been women for more than fifty years. I don't mean just the actresses. I mean the editors at the magazines, the stage managers, you name it."

"Why is that, Tommy?" Sister Maureen asked.

"Because women have always had an innate sense of attractive presentation: what turns a man on, and what turns a woman on. Believe it or not, women, who make up half of most couples, enjoy watching well-made porno flicks as much as men."

"Sort of like, 'It's the sizzle, not the steak?'" Jayson said.

"Exactly. People watching those kind of films want to see attractive, clean-looking, *young* well-built men and women. That way they can indulge their fantasies. But they want it done on clean sheets, in 'let's do it' surroundings. Test question: have any of you seen any 'blue' movies which were made in the last twenty years?"

All of them, shockingly including Sister Maureen, raised their hands.

"Used to be they were grainy black-and-white garbage. Today, production values are very close to Hollywood quality, as they should be since they use many of the same directors and cameramen that the big studios use. Most of the men and women who 'star' in those movies are no longer wacked-out druggies who'll do anything for their next 'fix.' They're every bit as gorgeous as the ones who were fortunate to make it to the next level."

"I'm satisfied," Ezra said. "What about food presentation?"

"St. Louis baby back ribs, suckling pig, prosciutto, pork sausage, kielbasa, every kind of anti-Muslim food you can imagine …"

"Uncle Joe?" Pete asked, picking up the lingo, referring to the retired Philadelphia boss.

"Uh-huh. Same guy who's doing the alcohol," Tommy replied. "We don't have to go the cocaine route, hashish, or any of that sh- … stuff. That's so common in the Middle East it would entice kids to go there. That's not what we're looking to do."

"So far, so good," Sister Maureen said. "If I could throw in an idea …?"

"Sister, you're the Chief of all the Indians. When the lady talks, everyone listens."

"The most effective way to really put the icing on the cake is to have young people, recruits and 'normals,' *laughing* at the ridiculousness of the whole thing. The perfect anti-recruiting tonic is to make ISIS look like the bozos they are. If *that* could somehow be put together… Even better, if it could be so over-the-top, politically incorrect, and in the worst bad taste …"

"I've got just the guy," Ezra said. "*And*, more important, the connections to get to him. He's not Israeli, but close enough. A bit long in the tooth but all of the mental parts still work fine."

"What do you mean, 'a bit long in the tooth?' 'Big' Mario Gigante's ninety-two and he's doin' just fine," Tommy said.

"The guy I have in mind is only a couple years younger. You ever heard of a guy named Melvin Kaminsky?"

Blank stares greeted him from every corner. It was JaysonElliott who caught on first. "Ho-ly shit, you can't mean …"

"I do mean, JaysonElliott."

"He's still alive?"

"And still working."

"The musical?"

"It's been delayed a few years but the last time he made it to Broadway …"

"Who are you two talking about?" Sister Maureen finally asked. "If it's who I think it is …?" She started humming the theme from the second highest-grossing western movie in history, then, incongruously, sang in a strong vice, "Springtime for Hitler and Germany …"

"Uh-huh," Ezra said. "None other than …"

"Mel Brooks!" she and Jayson said together.

"Can we get the cooperation of the Social Networks?"

"Not my department," the computer whiz replied. "But I'd say with the bad press the Islamic State has been getting all along, this is not a fight over whether Apple wants to protect some looney-tunes' privacy by bugging his phone. The tapes or programs or whatever else they feed out to the world are meant to be communicated to the largest audience they can get. If nobody knows where the knife is coming from, it shouldn't be a problem."

"How hard would it be?" Pedro asked.

"With today's technology, on a scale of one-to-ten, for anything but the Titan and the two Chinese top dogs it'd be fifty-one. With the Cray Titan, I'd say it's about a one."

"And the other part?" This from Maureen.

"Even easier. Have you ever noticed that on your personal computer programs, the right ads and the solicitations for money always seem to find you? You don't even have to punch in your name. Two days ago, I needed to buy something from Amazon. The minute I opened up my internet account and plugged in Amazon, it came up, 'Welcome back, JaysonElliott.' Even though you're one of seven billion people on the planet, Uncle Google can always find you."

# 24

The meeting took place at nine o'clock at night in a modest building far away from any inhabited settlement. From the outside, the structure appeared to have been bombed out some time ago. In fact, the place had been designated as a safe meeting house for disparate anti-Assad factions, almost none of which publicly collaborated with, or even acknowledged the validity of one another. Al-Qaeda, Al-Nusra, Hezbollah, and Islamic State envoys met from time to time to share information and to adjust their respective spheres of influence. On this night, there were four participants, al-Qaeda's Chief of Iraqi Operations, Ayman al-Zawahiri; his deputy; Mahmoud Abouzeid; Mufti Omar al-Qahtani, one of three main sharia leaders of the Islamic caliphate, whose job it was to instruct Muslims on how to swear allegiance to the caliph; and Abu Mohammed al-Zour, Abu Yahya al-Iraqi's executive secretary and assistant.

"Troubles?" Zawahiri commenced.

"Of course not, my brother," Zour assured his al-Qaeda rival and sometimes colleague.

"Then why did you call for this meeting?"

## PART FIVE – CHAPTER 24

"The usual reasons."

"The usual reasons are lack of money, which has never been a problem for ISIS, desertions from the ranks, dwindling recruitment, or fighting among the leadership."

"Well …"

"Zour, we've been comrades since our days together with Saddam. No matter how much the Syrian opposition is fragmented and fights among themselves, we are not stupid. So let us not hide behind the veil of intrigue and duplicity. The word throughout the region is that your Caliphate is getting the shit kicked out of them by some new, mysterious force whom no one seems to know."

"It may not be what you think, Mahmoud. You know how rumors get blown out of all proportion."

"Is it true or is it not true, Mufti? You're a man of Allah. I don't expect you to be untruthful." Zawahiri said.

"Neither entirely true nor entirely untrue, al-Zawahiri," the Mullah responded equivocally. "Yes, there is a strange new phenomenon. Our intelligence sources advise that at present it's directed only against the Caliphate and not against any other fighters for the freedom and the purity of Islam. We are taking steps …"

"Is it true or untrue that these 'mysterious phenomena,' as you call them, served you a banquet containing the roasted bodies of your own soldiers and their testicles?"

"I have heard such rumors. I have no firsthand knowledge."

"Caliph al-Zawahiri," Zour said. "May I be entirely truthful?"

"That would be appreciated," the al-Qaeda leader said, his tone neutral.

"We believe …"

"We?"

"Al-Aani, Abu Yahya al-Iraqi, my superior, and al-Asiri, who, like the Mufti, is a member of the Sharia Council."

"Go ahead."

"We believe there is an internal power struggle going on to replace al-Baghdadi."

"With whom? Turkmani? Anbari?"

"Neither, so far as we know. You're aware as well as I am that in this part of the world, it could be anyone from a Western stooge to an Assad ally, to someone wanting to bring back the rule of Saddam or Qaddafi."

Al-Zawahiri scratched his beard and looked thoughtful. An internal power struggle within the Islamic State could only help al-Qaeda. Since bin Laden's murder, ISIS had risen to prominence, pushing the older *jihadi* group into the shadows. Certainly the Islamic State, not dependent on Saudi Arabia for the vast bulk of its funding as was al-Qaeda, appeared flush with money and, more important, recruits to its cause. If ISIS was successful in its preeminence in Iraq and Syria and in its spreading terror network throughout the West, al-Qaeda could be downgraded into obscurity.

"On what evidence do you suspect such a plot?"

"People talk. Walls have ears."

"In other words, you have no evidence."

"In a manner of speaking," al-Zour replied. "However, we did not come to you to ask you to participate in our actions in any way. Neither money nor anything that would remotely tie al-Qaeda to our goals. I don't kid myself, Zawahiri, the demise of the Islamic State could rekindle interest in your own movement."

"What do you require of me?"

"Nothing more than a name and a private telephone number in Marrakech."

"And for that I receive …?"

"Ten thousand dollars, U.S. In cash."

"What do you know about Turki al-Binali, Mufti?"

"I don't trust him and I've never trusted him," Qahtani replied. "He came to us from Bahrain. He was expelled from the Emirates for his 'corrupt beliefs.' The real story I've heard is that he had rather 'unusual' tastes …. Young boys, young girls, it made no difference. The more perverse, the better."

"All in secret, of course?"

"When he can control it, although it's become quite an open secret of late. 'Coming out of the closet' as they say in the West. The Caliph looks the other way and becomes very hard of hearing when someone speaks ill of him, partly because Binali graduated with a degree in Islamic jurisprudence from one of the premier universities, which gives the Movement credibility in respected Muslim circles, and partly because whatever else he may be, he's a damned good recruiter."

"Not to mention he brought Saja al-Dulaimi to the party," Abu Yahya al-Iraqi, the caliph's bodyguard and al-Anbari's personal spy said, smiling knowingly.

"Amazing, isn't it, how every man, regardless of how strict a Muslim, is led around by his …"

"But not you, Holy Man?"

"I did not say that, al-Iraqi. I am as much flesh and blood as any man. Why did you specifically inquire about al-Binali, if I may ask?"

"The Caliph believes the heathen hordes who have chosen to attack our Movement in such a dishonorable manner have tarnished his reputation as a strong, unifying leader who is in total control. When something like that happens, the leader must demonstrate his power in a particularly dramatic way. The news of who and how must become known as quickly as possible to the largest cadre of the Islamic State, lest there be any doubt of al-Baghdadi's determination or his dominance."

"So Bengali must be the example?"

"He's high enough up the ladder. Would you rather it be you or me, Mufti?"

The following Monday an anonymous representative from the Islamic State telephoned a number in Marrakech, Morocco. The male voice at the other end said, "Yes?"

"Mister Khalili, my name is unimportant. I represent the Islamic State of Iraq and the Levant. I believe Ayman al-Zawahiri suggested to you that I might call?"

"He did."

"You understand the rules of our game?"

## PART FIVE – CHAPTER 24

"I do, Sir. In my business one needs to be both discreet and cautious."

"al-Zawahiri indicated to me that you deal in a particularly expensive and unique commodity?"

"That is so."

"Do you have such commodity available?"

"At present I have two, a male and a female, totally attuned to one another and delightful to watch."

"At what price?"

"Five hundred thousand United States dollars, apiece. One million for the matched pair."

"How would they feel about a third player? One who is completely unprejudiced."

"They've been trained to be very compliant."

"How old are they?"

"The male is nineteen, the female eighteen. Beautiful specimens."

"I'm not sure I will need them immediately. Might I propose a deposit to reserve their services?"

"One hundred thousand dollars a day, to a maximum of seven days. Should you exercise the option, the deposit would, of course, apply to the lease price."

"Fine, Mister Khalili. I shall wire the hundred thousand to your Swiss account each day. Will that be sufficient?"

"Quite."

"What if I decide to exercise the option?"

"The balance must be in my account before they're picked up."

"Excellent, Mister Khalili. Please hold them in readiness. I will transfer the funds to your account within the hour."

※

"My Caliph, I am beyond honored to be in your August presence once again. To what do I owe this supreme privilege?"

The man was oily, obsequious, but he'd fulfilled his purpose admirably. al-Baghdadi was not unaware of Turki al-Binali's reputation as a bisexual pederast and a disgusting pervert. Still, as the Supreme Leader, he needed to be above such things. Thus he masked his disdain.

"*Imam*," he said courteously. "You have been most effectively working for the greater good of the Islamic State for five years without a single moment to yourself."

"My Caliph, it is my honor and pleasure to serve you in whatever small, insignificant way I can. Has it been five years? It has seemed more like five minutes, my Lord."

"Ah, yes, *Imam* Binali, but even the Prophet Himself frowned on unrelieved slavery. You have more than earned a holiday. At a minimum, let us say a fortnight?"

"I would never have dreamed of such a luxury, My Leader."

"Of course, in our corner of the world, it might not be possible to, shall we say, indulge in one's natural wants and needs when one is within plain sight of the faithful every moment of every day."

"Majesty?"

"Come, come, Binali, we are men of the world, you and I. Might I suggest you take your holiday in a place where the Caliphate could arrange suitable companionship for you."

The scholar, who had been recruited to offer some religious legitimacy for the caliphate, but who, in reality, had no governing power, licked his lips in anticipation.

"Where would you suggest, My Caliph?"

"A friend of the Movement had offered a private villa in the countryside, far away from any neighbors, in the Republic of the Congo. We'll arrange to fly you into the friend's private airport …"

As the Lear pulled up to the terminal. Turki al-Binali watched in eager anticipation as the plane offloaded. The young people who deplaned were incredibly attractive, a boy who looked like a Greek god, and a girl who matched him in sensual feminine physical beauty. Their skin was a dusky, gold color. Binali felt a flush move up from his neck and down to his nether parts.

After the boy and girl had entered the villa, Binali flipped on the monitor which secretly recorded their every movement. No sooner had the bedroom door closed than the couple started kissing and fondling one another. Slowly, deliberately, they removed each other's clothing. Once there, they became oblivious to anything other than their own delicious lovemaking. It was as sexually titillating a performance as Binali had seen anytime in his life, and he longed to be part of it. He was already panting as he made for their bedroom.

The young man, Lehti, and his mate, Daiwanna, were delighted to welcome him to their nest, and suggested by smiles and gestures that Binali disrobe and join them. When he was undressed, both the boy and the girl rubbed fragrant oil all over his body, the young man tenderly caressing Binali's most sensitive parts, while the young woman rubbed her beautifully proportioned breasts against his chest. Their own sweat had an intense smell of love excretions, honey and almonds. Binali could not wait to be a part of this utter sexual abandon and immersed himself in their ecstasy.

Suddenly, something was very, very wrong. Binali felt a searing pain. He clutched at his eyes and tried to scream, but all that came out was a muffled gag. He felt a massive explosion in his stomach, and smelled the escape of his own excrement. His body twisted in a grotesque parody of sexual climax. Within moments, he was paralyzed. Binali knew he was dying, and knew with certainty that the Caliph of the Islamic State had sent him to his death.

The couple quietly arose from the bed, their job accomplished. They smiled at one another, left the corpse, and showered in the adjacent bathroom.

At just about that same time, al-Baghdadi's representative placed a call to Marrakech from an unidentified location in Libya. "Mister Khalili?"

"You've no worry, my friend," the familiar voice responded. "Pursuant to your instructions, a private aircraft will retrieve them within the hour."

"I don't mean to intrude on the details of our business, but just as a matter of personal interest, how do they manage to …?"

"Lehti and Daiwanna are *venefici*," the Moroccan replied. "Their tradition goes back six thousand years. From infancy, they were fed two of the world's deadliest poisons, first in minute amounts, then in increasing doses. By the time they were ten years old, their bodies were completely immune to those substances.

"Of course, anyone else partaking of the natural body juices of a *veneficus* or *venefica* will die a horrendous death within a very short time. Are you certain you won't have need of them again? After all, you have paid for them, and there are no refunds for returned merchandise."

"No, thank you, Mister Khalili. What will you do with them?"

"They will stay with me for a few days. Then, I will offer their services, again."

"Thank you once again, Mister Khalili." The phone disconnected.

Minutes later, the caller placed a second call to a number in Rabat. "Mister Dudley, there's a foul slave-trader, Hakim Khalili, who transacts his loathsome business in Marrakech. He has two particularly obscene love slaves whom he keeps in his home. Tomorrow morning, I want you to eliminate the three of them and burn the building where Mister Khalili keeps the records of his outrageous trade. His address is …"

# 25

THE past eighteen months had been a disaster for the Turkish Republic.

Atatürk International Airport, Istanbul's first airport, has one of the tightest security operations in Europe and the Near East. One needs a security pass even to get through the front doors of the eleventh busiest airport in the world. As it has been for more than twenty-five hundred years, Istanbul's position at the gateway to three continents, with one leg in Europe and the other in Asia, makes it one of the planet's most strategic locations.

That didn't stop three suicide bombers from attacking the airport, taking forty-two innocent lives, and wounding another two hundred thirty-nine bystanders. The United States Federal Aviation Administration immediately canceled all American flights into and out of Atatürk. Turkey, which was already suffering a fifteen percent fall-off in tourism since the year before, saw its main industry collapsing, threatening to be the worst year for in-country travel since the disastrous days of the Gulf War in 1991.

Three weeks after that, a segment of the Turkish military, which had quashed what they saw as *coup d'état,* military uprising in 1960, 1971, 1980, and 1997, attempted a coup against President Erdoğan's 14-year-old government which came perilously close to succeeding, despite the fact that it been a "colonel's coup" rather than one engineered by the current military leadership.

Later that month, the Islamic State stepped up its extraterritorial offensive.

The overthrow of the Muslim Brotherhood in Egypt and the installation of the al-Sisi government, which Turkey had condemned five years ago, but which appeared to be surviving and prospering, irked the Erdoğan government to no end.

Turkey had shown itself to be no more successful than France, Belgium, or the United States at defusing terrorist attacks from radical elements. Worse, Turkey itself was an Islamist nation. How in the world could a rogue *Islamic* state have turned cannibal against one of its own?

The only bright spot in a very dark month was that Turkey and Israel had reestablished diplomatic relations and, infinitely more important, financial and military ties.

The day had not started well for 48-year-old Mevlüt Çavuşoğlu. The constant hammering of EU and even the United States that Turkey's constant harsh actions against what they called "Freedom of the Press," was irksome and never-ending. Of course they'd never lived in the former land of the Sultans and later of Atatürk and seen how irresponsible a totally out-of-control bunch of malicious hooligans hell-bent on destroying a legitimately-elected government could be. Their clarion calls were getting stronger and more troublesome every day. The "Allah-damned Kurds," even worse than the Armenians with their push for international recognition of the falsely-labeled "genocide," were generating more kudos as "Freedom Fighters" every day. Why not call them what they really were? Out-and-out terrorists!

Two years ago, President Erdoğan had carefully orchestrated the departure of Prime Minister Davutoğlu. Before that, former president Abdullah Gül had been knocked off his perch, forced to resign. Each day it became more difficult for the current president to protect his backside. No doubt, the jackals were gathering. Çavuşoğlu himself had been criticized by one of the largest dailies, *Hürriyet,* for intervening in the municipal elections in Antalya, to keep that province in AKP hands. But Erdoğan was still president, the AKP, the ruling Justice and Development Party, was still firmly in control of Parliament, and if Erdoğan could only manage to steamroll the damned courts, the office of president would soon have the unlimited power he'd demanded.

As current Minister of Foreign Affairs and former president of the Parliamentary Assembly of the Council of Europe from 2010 to 2012, Çavuşoğlu, as spokesman for a government that was significantly less than universally popular outside of Turkey, found it increasingly difficult to walk the thin line separating his integrity in the international arena from his loyalty to his Party and its leader.

Turkey's minister of foreign affairs had just finished his light breakfast of rolls, olives, rose petal jelly, and hot tea when the telephone, his personal line, not his official line, rang.

The voice on the other end of the phone was as clear as if it came from the next room. "Mevlüt Effendim?"

"*Buyrun.*" (go ahead).

"Ezra Caen here. How are you, my friend?"

Despite his troubled mood, Çavuşoğlu grinned broadly as he recognized the voice of one of the few Israelis who had remained a reliable friend, even at a time when relations between their two countries had hit a low ebb after the 2010 *Mavi Marmara* incident.

"Shitty, if you must know, thank you very much," the minister replied. "What's on your mind, Ezra? Are you going to make my day better or worse?"

"How'd you like to trade Avigdor Lieberman for Davutoğlu, Gülen, and a few spare colonels?"

"We don't need to right now. Ahmet's out of my hair. The President's still in power. Lieberman's now your Secretary of Defense. Watch out, world!"

"That's not why I'm calling you," Ezra said. "I've been authorized to bring you into the circle of a lovely little conspiracy to get rid of the Islamic State, a conspiracy which, by the way, is sponsored by the Vatican."

"What is the *quid pro quo*, my friend?" the Turkish minister asked.

"Retribution," Ezra replied. "Our countries 'recognize' one another again. I know the position you've been in during the last few months. I'm sorry for the airport attack and the putative coup attempt, Mevlüt. But as awful as it was, it's taken a good bounce for Turkey, just as our 'remarriage of convenience' might help us both. Might I ask you as a personal friend to keep what I tell you under your hat?"

"Of course."

"Where and when can we meet? Out of the public eye?"

"Tbilisi. I'll be flying there tonight for one of those endlessly boring trade conferences in the morning, but we've got to show the happy face to our neighbor, even if that neighbor's embraced the Russians and is constrained in a 'Bear hug.'" There was no mistaking the meaning of that statement. Russia and Georgia enjoyed strong and amicable relations as long as the latter knew its place in the hierarchy.

"I've got the picture. No love lost between Putin and Erdoğan," Caen said. "I'd like to bring two friends along to fill in the details. One's a Roman Catholic nun and the other is a retired Mafia don, if you can believe that. How about Machakhela?" he continued, naming one of the more reasonable restaurants in Old Town. "What time does your meeting end?"

"Three in the afternoon. I return to Ankara at eight."

"Perfect. We'll fly in on Turkish Flight 382 and meet you at six at Machakhela."

෨෬

"I'd heard rumors about that over-the-hill bunch of Mafiosi and their 'Wrecking Crew.' So they really exist?"

"Big time, Mevlüt. They're shaking up the Islamic State in ways you would not believe, and, as a devout Muslim, you might not *want* to believe," Caen said, spooning the last of his *Kharcho*, chicken seasoned and seared before being tucked into a sauce made of five Georgian spices, garlic, cilantro, walnuts and sour cherries, onto chewy, savory *shoti* bread. He mentioned some of the antics of the Wrecking Crew without disclosing the names of the deceased.

When Sister Maureen told the foreign minister what they'd planned, Çavuşoğlu practically choked on his *Mtsvadi, Georgian shish kebab.*

"We'll need your help in two ways. The first is for remote, not readily identifiable relay points," Caen added. "Can you get government approval?"

"Can I get what?"

"Government approval."

"Can I get what?" the foreign minister repeated, smilingly emphasizing the last word to indicate that the Turkish government did not know and did not want to know of such an activity. He added, "Of course it might be better if the relay points were just over the Turkish border, Kapitan Andreevo in Bulgaria, Kipoi in Greece, Yerevan, Armenia, and Batumi. Anything else, my friends?"

"There is, Mevlüt," Caen said. "It's a tossup whether Turks or Israelis are the best soldiers in the world. For our purposes, it really doesn't matter, since there'll be no identifiable uniforms. This operation will be a three-prong knockout punch. The social media blitz will be ongoing for as long as we need the programs. We need five thousand of your shock troops on the ground to come across the border from the northwest. Another five thousand of ours will come up from the south. No one needs to know who they are. Those troops will do what they have to do and be gone seventy-two hours later. There'll be air support strikes from aircraft bearing markings no one has seen in, let's just say a long while."

"Dare I hazard a guess …?"

"You may, but I won't ruin the surprise by giving you an answer. The pilots and the planes will take off from Jordan, Saudi Arabia, Lebanon, Egypt, and Iran. They'll return to a different country where their original livery will be repainted onto the aircraft within those seventy-two hours."

"Where, if I may ask…?"

"You may not. Ask me no questions and I'll tell you no lies."

"Do your people know we'd be involved?"

"Of course."

"The 'Wrecking Crew?'"

"Yes," Tommy Aiello chimed in. "One more thing. Your shock troops will be furnished with small gifts for the enemy."

"Gifts?"

"Ten thousand red golf balls with the Turkish star and crescent painted on them."

※

Dennis O'Brien and Sister Maureen had just finished their first session with Mel Brooks, which had been congenial and filled with laughter during the entire four hours. Brooks had not lost one iota of his humor, his maniacal brilliance, or his boundless energy. They'd quickly selected the vehicles they thought would best serve their purpose: *Blazing Saddles, Young Frankenstein,* and, of course, *The Producers*, both the original and the post-Broadway version.

They culled the most outrageous parts of those movies, then, through modern technology, reworked them so they would specifically target, satirize, and humiliate the Islamic State's message to the maximum degree possible.

※

Tommy Aiello, who'd been used to the skin racket in his earlier life, met with the various producers and outlined exactly what they needed, and the patriotic uses that would be made of the product. The assortment of what they received ran the gamut from titillating to positively disgusting. "Different strokes for different folks," Aiello told his confreres.

JaysonElliott coordinated the hack-and-broadcast program perfectly. To ensure that there was a moving target so sophisticated it would take months, if not years, for the Islamic State to decipher and counteract what the Wrecking Crew had planned, communications posts, coordinated through the Cray Titan, were sited in three hundred locations in fifty-four different nations.

Meanwhile, FBI special agents met with representatives and experts of every major social media to determine the days of the week and times of the day when the largest number of "hits" historically occurred from 2011 to the current date.

The field marshal, the Generalissimo, the fourteen generals, Ezra Caen, Manucher Tabrizi, the FBI representatives, certain insiders, and those international representatives who'd been briefed on what was about to happen, held their final meeting on November 15. Sister Maureen opened the meeting with the words, "Okay, folks, I guess I should say 'Break a leg.' Tomorrow morning, it's **Show Time!**"

After congratulations all around, she left the room, dignity intact, while the less formal, alcohol-lubricated celebration of what they all hoped would be the most successful strike ever made against the Islamic State, ensued.

# 26

THURSDAY, November 16, promised to be a balmy 66° Fahrenheit in Mosul and two degrees higher in Al-Raqqah, Syria. An early winter's chill had resulted in temperatures ranging from twenty-two to twenty-five degrees cooler throughout Western Europe.

Musaf al-Ibrahim, who had previously been known as Steve Evans when he'd grown up in Poughkeepsie, New York, had risen at five in the morning, glanced out the splotchy window of his tiny cold-water walk-up flat in east London's Whitechapel District, watching with approval as young Muslim Patrol members goaded and abused the few occupants of the street at that hour, admonishing them to obey *Sharia*, Islamic law.

As was his custom, al-Ibrahim washed his hands in the filthy sink, lowered himself to a small prayer rug, and bowed in the direction of the nearest Mosque before commencing his morning prayers. Afterward, he glanced at his watch. 5:40. The morning program would be simulcast on YouTube and Facebook in precisely three minutes. He pushed the power button. His trusty ASUS UX-305 sprang to life with a cheery, "Welcome back, Musaf al-Ibrahim."

## PART FIVE – CHAPTER 26

His fingers navigated to YouTube. He quickly typed in "Islamic State current broadcast." Unknown to him, just as it was unknown to those who regularly resorted to their own personal instruments to protect their privacy, al-Ibrahim's computer had its own "fingerprint" which was traceable from anywhere in the world. "Big brother" knew what Steve Evans bought, where and from whom he bought it, and what advertisements or programs most drew his attention. The purveyors of his custom knew his tastes almost better than he did himself.

The familiar face of the ISIS leader came onscreen. After a brief introductory prayer in Arabic, of which al-Ibrahim / Evans could understand perhaps every fifth word, the leader said in English, "Welcome, my English-speaking brothers of the spirit. May your day be filled with ..."

A sudden momentary blackout interfered with what al-Ibrahim / Evans was watching, causing him to curse involuntarily. Only two or three seconds later the program resumed.

Only it wasn't the program he'd been watching moments ago.

Two naked men, one middle-aged and one in his early twenties, Steve Evans' age, engaged in an orgy of lovemaking involving every orifice and organ in or appendant to their bodies. To a conservative heterosexual the graphic scene would have been disgusting beyond tolerance. But Steve Evans / Musaf al-Ibrahim had secret tastes which he'd never revealed to anyone outside his own bedroom.

He watched, transfixed, feeling a rush of sexual adrenaline coursing through his body. He moved his right hand lower ...

Just as he approached climax, the screen went dark for two more seconds before the black standard of the Islamic State flashed on the screen, followed immediately by a huge black letters on a white background. His eyes, drawn as if by magnets, followed the message as it scrolled up.

> WELCOME STEVE EVANS / MUSAF AL-IBRAHIM!
> YOU BELIEVE WHAT YOU HAVE BEEN WATCHING HAS BEEN SPONSORED BY THE ISLAMIC STATE OF IRAQ AND THE LEVANT.
> WRONG!
> YOU'VE BEEN WATCHING A MOVIE SPECIALLY GEARED TO YOUR TASTES BY THE F.B.I. WE KNOW YOU'VE SECRETLY LOVED IT.
> YOU MIGHT WANT TO THINK TWICE BEFORE BECOMING MORE INVOLVED WITH THE ISLAMIC STATE FOR WE'LL BE WATCHING YOU.
> HAVE A NICE DAY.

Steve Evans barely made it to the toilet before he threw up.

Magrebh Rabati, who'd changed his name to Lucien Brenot when he'd emigrated to Brussels from Morocco six years ago, had invited fourteen specially selected young men, ideal potential recruits, to his capacious residence in one of the Belgian capital's better non-Muslim neighborhoods.

He'd been advised two nights before that the largest major recruiting program in the last four months, would take place on November 16.

In order to evade the ever-more sophisticated watchdogs, whom ISIS knew would be trying to jam or interfere with the Islamic State's powerful broadcasts, the Organization's propaganda machine copied a page out of the handbook of the most hated enemy of all, the Allah-damned Israelis, who changed the departure times and routes of their El Al flights from various world capitals and major cities to Ben Gurion Airport only a few minutes before the flights were scheduled to take off. The ISIS program would be broadcast on *WeChat* at precisely 10:17 a.m. in the Central European Time Zone. It would simultaneously be broadcast around the world.

Brenot had hooked his computer to a three thousand watt projector aimed at a large screen with the most advanced speaker system he could afford. At 10:16, he dimmed the lights on the room.

A minute later, the familiar face and voice of Caliph Abu bakr al-Baghdadi, worldwide leader of the Islamic State of Iraq and the Levant, appeared on the large screen.

"Greetings and peace be with you," he began in Arabic with French, English, and German subtitles. "We are delighted and privileged that you are joining our Great Struggle to purify and bring *Sharia* to the entire world. Today we will show you the respect and admiration we have acquired in every country on earth and why we have captured the hearts and minds of every right-thinking follower of Allah, praise be His glorious Name."

There was a smooth transition as the large screen darkened, then lightened, portraying a dozen ISIS soldiers standing behind the same number of kneeling, blindfolded men, readying to slice off the heads of the terrified apostates whose religious zeal had been deemed wanting.

Suddenly, there was the explosive, unmistakable sound of the loud passing of gas, followed immediately by the sound of several men passing wind, one after the other – nothing more nor less than the technologically updated remake of the "I think you boys have had enough beans" campfire scene that had shocked and titillated millions of people who'd watched Mel Brooks' *Blazing Saddles* some forty-two years before.

Brenot, struck like a bludgeoned ox, stood transfixed, unable to shut off the hypnotic scene on the screen.

The gaseous emissions were followed by every one of the killers, and many of the victims, coughing and holding their noses. The would-be murderers dropped their swords. Using their hands and even their *kaffiyehs,* they vigorously waved away what appeared on screen to be an awful stench.

Try as he might, Brenot was completely helpless to stop the barrage of raucous laughter that filled the room. Soon the giggling was joined by several would-be recruits pinching their lips together and blowing air out their mouths in imitation of passing gas. A few watchers managed to produce their own gaseous explosions.

While this was going on, the screen went dark, then lightened again on a different scene. In another Mel Brooks hit of the 1970s, *Young Frankenstein*, a grotesque monster, the creation of Doctor Frankenstein, portrayed by cockeyed, misshapen English actor Marty Feldman, dances and "almost" sings *Puttin' On the Ritz*. The scene was rebroadcast that morning with a significant difference: the head atop Feldman's body was easily recognizable as that of Abu bakr al-Baghdadi, even with his technologically realigned, grossly misshapen face. al-Baghdadi was jovially, if spasmodically, "dancing" to the same song that had been written by the American Jewish Tin Pan Alley composer Isaac Bailin, better known to the world as Irving Berlin, back in 1927.

By this time, any attempt to dissuade the audience from viewing the screen was doomed to failure. Fourteen twenty-something men in Brenot's residence and Allah-knew how

## PART FIVE – CHAPTER 26

many thousands of watchers around the world raptly watched the scene play out, laughing as loud and uproariously as their forbears had done while watching the second highest grossing "western" in history.

The screen went dark, then lit up again as a message stood in bold relief on the screen:

### DEAR ISIS RECRUITS:

**AS THE "GREAT LEADER" HAS TOLD YOU, THE UNITED NATIONS OF THE FREE WORLD ARE SHOWING YOU EXACTLY HOW MUCH "RESPECT AND ADMIRATION" ISIS HAS ACQUIRED IN EVERY COUNTRY ON EARTH. KEEP WATCHING, ENJOY OUR "GIFT" TO YOU, AND ASK YOURSELF IF THIS IS WHAT YOU <u>REALLY</u> WANT.**

**LOVE FROM YOUR FRIENDS IN "<u>THE WRECKING CREW</u>."**

What followed was even more bizarre. The "Springtime for Hitler" show stopper from *The Producers* segued into a large group of masked, hooded figures in *ersatz* ISIS "uniforms" reminiscent of Ku Klux Klan robes, dancing, gesticulating, and singing in Arabic (with English, French, and German subtitles) a song which had been popularized in 1978 by The Village People …

"Young man, there's no need to feel down, I said
Young man, pick yourself off the ground, I said
Young man, 'cause you're in a new town
There's no need … to … be … unhappy
Young man, there's a place you can go, I said

Young man, when you're short on your dough, You can
Stay there … and I'm sure you will find
Many ways … to … have … a good time . . . . . It's fun to stay at the
**Y.M.C.A. …. Y.M.C.A.**
They have everything there for you men to enjoy
You can hang out with all the boys …"

As the song continued, the screen once again filled with a rolling message:

**WHAT'S YOUR LIFE WORTH?**
**LIFE'S TOO PRECIOUS TO GIVE IT AWAY**
**FOR THOSE WHO THINK ONLY OF THEMSELVES!**
**THE WORLD IS A FAMILY OF GOOD PEOPLE.**
**REMAIN A PART OF IT.**
**"THE WRECKING CREW."**

※

Al-Baghdadi seethed inwardly. If this was not nipped in the bud, and pretty damned quickly, it could wreak incalculable havoc on the entire Movement. The man they called the Caliph had not gotten to where he was by being naïve or a fool or both. He'd proved a master at propaganda, one of the world's true experts at manipulation by and through social media. Someone of al-Baghdadi's character was completely aware that the worst enemy, the worst nightmare of a movement built on fanaticism, was satire: to be the butt of uncontrollable laughter _at_ rather than _with_ the Islamic State. Al-Baghdadi knew exactly how serious this threat was.

## PART FIVE – CHAPTER 26

Within half an hour, every one of his major deputies desperately contacted every nerve center of ISIS's worldwide operations with the same message: find out where the sacrilegious, abominable pseudo-recruiting program was coming from; obliterate, destroy, and block it; prepare programs to counter it immediately; get our own I.T. men and every ISIS-controlled or monitored computer in the world to start flooding every social media possible with new, or even old, dependable propaganda, "education" content.

Less than an hour later, every one of these deputies reported the same bleak message back to the Caliphate's headquarters:

1. We cannot locate the computer or computers that have hacked into our system.
2. We cannot block out the infamous program, no matter how sophisticated our track-and-destroy equipment.
3. Whoever is behind this abomination had traced all of our controlled computers and has locked us out of each social media network; and, worst of all,
4. The false program appears to be spreading much faster than we can control it.

The question of what to do to avoid a nuclear meltdown of the Islamic State was on the mind and the lips of every member of the Shura Council, the Provincial Council, the Military Council, the Security and Intelligence Council, the Religious Affairs Council, the Financial Council, and the all-important Media Council.

And there were no satisfactory answers.

For the first time since the accession of the Islamic State of Iraq and *al-Sham*, a mood of panic pervaded the highest echelons of leadership.

The impossible, the unimaginable, while by no means a certainty, began to show signs of becoming a very real possibility. A sense of impending doom, hitherto unthinkable, hovered like a gigantic storm cloud on the horizon.

※

Within three hours of its initial broadcast, the program seen by Brenot and his audience, which had led to chaos in the Islamic State leadership, had gone viral. From YouTube to Facebook, the video had raced around the planet at the speed of light. No matter what the Islamic State tried to do to stop, block, or destroy it, their I.T. people were, to use an abominable phrase, "hamstrung" at every turn. Nearly as quickly as it permeated the social media, the program spread to the airwaves from commercial and cable television to the farthest reaches of the internet.

Within six hours of the initial broadcast, law enforcement officers throughout Europe, the Americas, Asia, and North Africa, alerted by the "fingerprints" of almost ever computer who'd tuned in to what was being hailed as "The Mel Brooks Follies of 2018," as well as to other Wrecking Crew-sponsored fakepath ISIS productions, swooped down on every computer they could find that had tuned in. Thousands were arrested, thousands more were detained. Not only computers, but weapons caches were seized and destroyed at an unprecedented rate.

For the first time since the rise of the Islamic State, turncoat informers far outnumbered recruits. The more ISIS tried to combat the destruction, the worse luck they had.

`But the worst was yet to come.

# 27

An hour before dawn on November 17, every border checkpoint leading from Turkey into Iraq or Syria was slammed shut. All roads into Syria from the south and west were likewise closed.

As ISIS troops awakened in their strongholds, they found themselves surrounded by thousands of armed troops wearing no discernible or identifiable uniforms. So rapidly did these troops move that pockets of Islamic State defenders were cut off both from their supply lines and from their compatriots. ISIS troops were herded into the desert, far away from their bases.

Moments later, a low roar issued from the skies over ISIS-held territory as World War II propeller-driven aircraft, Messerschmitt Bf-109s, English Spitfires, American P-51 Mustangs, and Japanese Zeroes, made runs less than fifteen hundred feet over the heads of the startled ISIS troops, dropping an almost infinite number of multicolored golf balls.

Less than three minutes later, terror from the skies erupted as the unmistakable scream of advanced jet aircraft shattered the late November morning calm, dropping incendiary bombs with pinpoint accuracy over every known Islamic State base or camp in both Syria and Iraq. While the Islamic State could not mount a single challenge to these devils from the sky, ISIS radar traced them as coming from Saudi Arabia, Jordan, Egypt, Lebanon, Kuwait, and Qatar. Not a single plane originated in Israel.

Each of the over one hundred fifty aircraft bore the insignia of Hitler's *Luftwaffe*, from black swastikas on the tails to white-coated black crosses in the center of the fuselages, to yellow nose nacelles: all of the markings used by the dreaded *Luftwaffe* at the height of its terrifying power.

The "battle" was over two hours after it started.

"This is Christiane Amanpour in the World Service of CNN. In less than twenty-four hours, the world has witnessed the greatest victory of the forces of good since the end of the Second World War …"

"This is Anderson Cooper. We may never know or properly analyze how it all came together, but the back of the Islamic State has been incurably broken. While movements such as ISIS, al-Qaeda, and the Hydra-headed monsters of nihilism and destruction can never be totally eliminated as long as there is a single human being filled with the pus of human hatred and despair, today marked a significant turning point in the War against those who would take away the basic, universal freedoms to which every human being is entitled."

CNN's Fareed Zakariah reported, "Last night, the world finally put the threat of ISIS into perspective. We gave up the fighting, the fear, the things that divide us, to realize we still knew how to laugh, and, after all, laughter is the best medicine. Today, we came together long enough to realize that the things that separate us are so small compared to those things we all share in common: the simple need to live in peace, without disturbance from outside forces. The simple need to love, to work together, to raise our children so that their world will be a better place because we inhabited the earth. The Jewish saying *Tikkun Olam* says it best: to repair the world."

"I'm Wolf Blitzer. Today the knockout punch to the violent Islamic State was delivered in the most dramatic and meaningful way imaginable... forces from many countries came together on the ground. Aircraft came from the skies of every Arab country in the neighborhood, flown by Jews, Muslims, Christians, Europeans, Americans, human beings from around the world. Some of these planes were ancient relics from another age. More than one hundred-fifty were Israeli-built *Kfir,* supersonic 'Lion Cubs' flown by Israel's erstwhile 'sworn enemies.' Every one of these aircraft had one thing in common. They bore the insignia of the Third Reich, the symbol of the Empire of Evil which almost destroyed the world. Only this time, they redeemed the free world. This is Wolf Blitzer from CNN headquarters in Atlanta ..."

" ... Laurent Ruquier, Paris ..."

"... Kate Adie, London ..."

" ... Hu Shuli, Beijing..."

"... Shereen Bhan, Mumbai ..."

"... Gidi Weitz, Tel Aviv ..."

"...Tom Friedman, New York City ..."

The final commentator, returned from the dead through the medium of technology, concluded, "And this is Walter Cronkite, CBS Evening News, wishing you all a very good evening indeed."

# 28

Abu Bakr al-Baghdadi had once served as Imam of a few mosques outside of Baghdad. For the past two-and-a-half years he'd been the Caliph of a grand Islamic State that stretched over a large portion of two significant Middle East countries; head of a Movement whose tentacles stretched from Indonesia to Morocco, throughout Europe and into the United States. His domain, which had been called the latest incarnation of the Empire of Evil, had engendered fear and caused a political upheaval, had collapsed. Baghdadi stood on a small hill east of Al-Raqqah, forlornly surveying the remains of what had been.

His great plan to bring Sharia to the world, to ensure that the purity of Allah's law would govern relations between mankind for the next thousand years, had been reduced to smoldering ashes, ruins as far as his eye could see.

Yesterday his incipient domination of the planet had been on the ascendant. Despite some minor losses attributable to an abominable bunch of hooligans who called themselves "the Wrecking Crew," the Islamic State had seemed more viable than ever. Istanbul, then Paris, then London, then New York City were within his grasp. He was not yet forty-six years old, with at least another forty years of power ahead of him.

## PART FIVE – CHAPTER 28

His most trusted lieutenants, who'd proved their endless devotion and loyalty to the State to be as thin as water, had deserted the Cause in the middle of the night, disappearing into the vast desert wasteland, abandoning even each other. Baghdadi, as a student of history, was keenly aware that it had always been that way. Today's conquering hero, today's savior of the world, would be cast into obloquy, paraded in shame before a jeering crowd or killed in the most hideous way imaginable after a mock "trial" on trumped up "charges" of "crimes against humanity."

At least there would be some monument to his greatness that would long outlive him: the Movement at its zenith had brought down and obliterated a thousand archaic symbols of false religion, another thousand sacrilegious "shrines." The heathens had condemned the Islamic State for "wholesale destruction of World Heritage sites," studiously ignoring that throughout history iconoclasts of every stripe had similarly removed the cancer of such pseudo-religious piles of rock or scandalous mountains of paper from the purer earth.

Baghdadi's reverie was interrupted by a lone figure on the horizon, who moved determinedly forward. As the figure came closer, Baghdadi saw that the man, who was his own height but much younger, was alone. He appeared to be unarmed. The stranger whistled a tune unknown to the now-Caliph of nowhere and casually tossed a single red golf ball from one hand to the other.

Coming closer, the man pocketed the golf ball and held his hands out, palms forward, to show he did not intend to do harm.

"Abu Bakr al-Baghdadi?"

The Caliph nodded but said nothing.

"My name is Pedro Sanchez," the man said in simple Arabic.

Baghdadi, recognizing that the stranger would not be able to converse much farther in that language, addressed him in English. "I suppose your army is over the next rise waiting for me to make an unexpected move."

"They might be or they might not be. Does it matter?"

"What do you mean?"

"I am unarmed. You could kill me with a dagger or a small handgun. My associates, even if they are just over the next hill, could annihilate you within seconds afterward, but I would not be any the less dead."

Baghdadi thought of what Sanchez had said. If Baghdadi had been armed, he could indeed snuff out of the life of this infidel. Perhaps he wouldn't even need a weapon to do this, since Baghdadi was a physically powerful man, in the prime of life despite the low station to which he had sunk.

"You are a brave man, Mister Sanchez, and a thoughtful one. You knew who I was as you approached me?"

"I did."

"How?"

"You're not exactly an unknown entity. You did not attempt to hide who you are. There's a certain amount of courage to be said for that. I can't say the same for your associates."

"They were …?"

"Rounded up as they fled your headquarters under cover of darkness. You stayed until the bitter end. Why?"

"Because I led a cause I believe in. You are part of this group which calls itself 'the Wrecking Crew?'"

"I am."

"You are how old? Twenty, twenty-one?"

"I'll be twenty-two in four months."

"The same age as so many of our soldiers," Bagdhadi said pensively. "Do you have any idea why so many rallied to our cause?"

"From what we've been told, a misguided religious belief."

"'We?' You are American, then?"

"Yes."

"Then you can never have experienced what those who gather to our banner have endured. You live in a land of perpetual plenty, no doubt privileged to enjoy every aspect of material wealth, while your nation is morally bankrupt, flailing about in a wilderness of comfort with no real direction. A rudderless ship headed nowhere."

"You think that's true about all Americans, Mister al-Baghdadi?"

"I have never known it to be otherwise."

"Perhaps you might think differently if I tell you my story."

༺༻

"So now you intend to take me prisoner?"

"What's to be gained by that?"

"You'd be a great hero in the West. The man who singlehandedly captured the leader of the Islamic State and brought him to 'justice.'"

"Would it be justice or would it simply be retribution?"

"What difference does it make?"

"I heard somewhere that if you save one life, it's as though you've saved the universe, but if you destroy a life, you've destroyed the universe."

The ISIS leader stood silent for a few moments. Then he said, "There may be merit in what you say, Mister Sanchez. You've shown yourself to be a brave man. Now you appear to be a righteous man as well. That's not to say we agree on much, if anything. It's simply a gesture of genuine respect from one man to another."

"Do you see anything to be gained by my taking you prisoner? Or, for that matter, trying to kill you?"

"Not for me in any event," the erstwhile head of the Islamic State said, smiling.

"Nor for me, either, Mister Baghdadi. I'm told you've been responsible for a number of deaths. So have I, but I don't think whether you live or die should be on my hands. That's between you and your Allah. In time, you and He might discuss that. So, Mister Baghdadi, my response to your invitation to capture you and haul you back to wherever you think I should, is 'Thanks, but no, thanks.' I think it's time for me to return to my people, Mister Baghdadi. I wish you well for the rest of your life. You might just think about making life easier for those around you. Goodbye, Mister Baghdadi."

"Goodbye, Mister Sanchez."

Abu Bakr al-Baghdadi stood still for several moments, watching Pedro depart. Sanchez did not look back. "You are a good man, Pedro Hernandez Sanchez," the Caliph said softly.

"May we meet again in Heaven." Baghdadi turned and walked slowly back toward Al-Raqqah.

"Did you bring back Baghdadi?"

"No, Sir."

"Why not?"

"Wrong guy, General Tommy. Turned out to be someone who looked a bit like him from far away, but up close, *nada*."

"You're a very poor liar, Pedro," Aiello said gently. "On the other hand, you're a very compassionate man. May I ask you why you didn't?"

"I remember a story you told me a couple of months ago, General …"

"Tommy."

"Tommy, then. You said that a wolf, whenever he knows he's lost the fight, bares his throat to the other wolf as a sign of complete submission. The winner of the fight is honor bound not to kill the loser once he's given up like that. The guy I met out there, maybe he was Baghdadi, maybe he was someone else, I'll never know. He was defeated, he knew it, and he was ready to accept whatever he had coming to him. Maybe someone else will do what I was supposed to do. Maybe the man I spoke with will just walk out into the desert somewhere and take up preachering in some tiny, out-of-the-way hole where he might even do a little bit of good for someone. Whether he lives or dies is up to God or some other people. But I'm not God and I don't see having the power of life or death over someone as something I want."

"You know, Son, I had that power for many years."

"Did it make you feel good?"

"Hard to say, Pedro. I thought it did, at least for awhile. I thought it proved something when I counted the number of beautiful women I slept with. It took me almost eighty years to realize none of that mattered. I'd end up the same, whether I was the best man who ever lived or the worst. Five, maybe ten years after we're gone who remembers we even lived? I wonder if anyone will ever even visit my gravestone, although I'd like to think someone might. Hey, Captain, that sounds pretty melodramatic, doesn't it?

"If you say so, General. Are you driving or am I?"

The long road from northeastern Syria to **Şanlıurfa**, Turkey wound through a semi-desert. Both Sanchez and Aiello were thankful that it was November and that they did not have to turn on the air conditioner in the Land Rover.

Having little better to do, the two men talked incessantly on the way back to the Turkish city of half a million which, according to legend, had been the patriarch Abraham's birthplace.

"So where do you go from here, Pedro?"

"If you'd asked me that question eight months ago, I might have said 'Back to Soledad Prison.' Today, thanks to what happened, the first place I'm going is back to a very good woman, the mother of my baby girl. The first thing I'm going to do is make an honest woman of her so we can start on a little

## PART FIVE – CHAPTER 28

brother or sister. I'm not forgetting that this gig gave me an all-expense-paid college education. That's going to take a few years. Then, who knows?"

"You ever considered becoming an Army officer?"

"Yes, Tommy, I have. On the other hand, I've had a bellyful of war, so I'd like to explore other options. Heck, I'm not even twenty-two. A year ago there was nothing ahead of me but a big, black hole. Today ..."

Tommy "Legs" Aiello sighed deeply. "I'd give a lot to be even twice as old as that."

"I'm sorry, General. That was awfully inconsiderate of me to just rag on about myself."

"Not a problem, Kid. You think I didn't say much the same thing back when I was your age? Hell, when you're twenty-two and full of piss and vinegar, the whole world is yours to conquer. The girls are all young and beautiful with tits that point up at the sky and you can get hard, and stay hard, at the snap of a finger. It all goes by so damn quickly..."

They rode awhile longer before Pedro broke the silence.

"You've got to admit, Tommy, it was one helluva last hurrah for you. It seems such a waste to put you back out to pasture. If anyone proved that old age and treachery could defeat youth and vigor every time, it was you."

"Yeah, I've been thinking the same thing. But guess what? It might not happen that fast."

"What do you mean?"

"Sister Maureen cornered me the day after they announced the collapse of ISIS. She's been asked by the President to serve as a Special Projects Officer, to come up with ideas of what needs fixing in our country and then do something about it. She wondered if I'd be interested in a job as her Deputy for evaluating how American society deals with Organized Crime and how we could better deal with that problem." He chuckled. "Can you imagine, *me*, a retired Capo di Capi being a stooge for the Feds without even having to snitch on my old friends?"

"At least, it would keep you off the streets and give you an honest way of making living rather than sponging off the government for your seventy-five thousand tax free a year."

"Yeah, but can you imagine, I'd have to become a 'suit' and show up everyday for work?"

"And you didn't do that back when you were 'Capo'ing' or whatever they called it?"

"Son," Aiello said jovially, "just remember, everyone likes a little 'ass' but nobody likes a smartass."

"Dennis, I couldn't be more delighted for you," Ezra said. "No more fear of being put out to pasture. Full retirement next year and the day after you get your gold watch you start your seven year ironclad contract as a strategic consultant to the National Security Council."

"The good thing is I get to remain based inside the Beltway and I get to run my own shop. The downside is I've got to take care of my own taxes and try to find as many loopholes as I possibly can. Thank God for Barry Dolowich."

"I met him once. Sharp Jewish C.P.A. In his case, the initials don't stand for 'Cleaning, Pressing, and Alterations.'" This brought a laugh from the FBI agent.

## PART FIVE – CHAPTER 28

"What about you, Ezra? You've certainly earned a helluva lot more feathers in your cap from this."

"What about me, Dennis?" the Israeli replied. "I'll just remain semi-retired, puttering around in my little garden, trying to keep myself out of mischief …"

"Yeah, as if you think I'd buy that. One of the most exciting women in the universe, everyone everywhere seeming to clamor for your services …"

"Not fair," Caen rejoined. "I've always been known as 'the plodder.' Why should I change things now?"

"Uh-huh. And pigs fly."

"Speaking of which, did you know that early on, the Jewish National Fund prohibited pigs in Israel? But most of the rest of the world can't do without their morning bacon, or holiday ham. Some enterprising Jewish farmers found a way around the injunction against raising pigs on the land of Israel. Every pig from the day it was born lived on a wooden platform several inches above the ground. Thus, the porkers never touched the 'land' of Israel. At least that's the legend. Whether it's true or not, I don't know, but pig farming is still a multimillion dollar industry in the Holy Land."

"Chuey, you big-mouthed little shit!"

"Fuck off, *muchacho*."

Both men grinned at one another. It was their first day at Cal State University Monterey Bay. Pedro had successfully argued for Garza to be enrolled in the Wrecking Crew's university program, despite his rocky start "on the wrong side." Since then, the two of them had surmounted their past and become genuinely fond of one another.

"What's your major, amigo?" Pedro asked.

"Same as yours, 'don't know yet.' But however I do end up, my friend, it's thanks to you. I could have gone the other way so easily. Have you and Angie started on number two yet?"

"Hey, it's only been two months since the wedding. Give us a little time to ourselves. By the way, any truth to the rumor that …?"

"Uh huh. Who'd ever have thought I'd end up with a very special lady like that?"

"Beats playing with yourself."

"Hey, Pedro?"

"Yeah?"

"Go fuck yourself."

# 29

NEITHER of the two middle-aged men, each wearing nondescript slacks and open-necked shirts looked particularly memorable. Truth to tell, they would have disappeared into the woodwork, had they been at a social event. They spoke quietly as they walked among the magnificent ruins at Baalbek in Lebanon's Beq'a Valley.

"Did you know that the Temple of Bacchus is larger than the Parthenon?"

"Supposed to be the best preserved ancient temple in the world."

"That might be, but the Temple of Jupiter's the one all the tourists come to see. So you survived and avoided the manhunt?"

"Thanks in no small part to your people."

"My country or my Crew?"

"Both, I suppose. Either way, I owe you my life."

"No more terrorism in your future?"

"I've been there, done that."

They were silent for a few moments. Then Ezra continued. "Bad guys have turned into good guys throughout history.

Menachem Begin, Nelson Mandela, Yassar Arafat, George Washington …"

"George Washington?"

"The British sure as hell didn't think of him as anything but a terrorist. Today's terrorist sometimes becomes tomorrow's Statesman."

"You said you had a proposition?"

"I did. Thanks for coming here, Abu. You ever heard of a guy named Otto Skorzeny?"

"No."

"Nobody remembers him today. For that matter, when you count how many people have lived on Earth since the beginning of time, the number of people anyone remembers ten years after they died is minuscule. He was a bad guy who, in the end, did something of value."

"Who was he?"

"Otto Skorzeny joined Austria's branch of the Nazi Party in 1931, when he was 23. When Hitler invaded Poland in 1939, Skorzeny volunteered for the SS Panzer division, Hitler's personal bodyguard force. In September 1943, he led a group of commandos who flew engineless gliders to an Italian mountaintop resort to rescue Benito Mussolini, and helped put him back in power.

"In September 1944, when Hungary's Admiral Horthy was on the verge of suing for peace with Russia, Skorzeny led a contingent of Special Forces into Budapest to kidnap Horthy and replace his government with the more hard-line Fascist Arrow Cross. That regime went on to kill or deport tens of thousands of Hungarian Jews who had managed to survive the war up to that point.

## PART FIVE – CHAPTER 29

"During that same year, Skorzeny handpicked 150 soldiers to fend off the Allies after they landed in Normandy. Skorzeny dressed his men in captured U.S. uniforms, and procured captured American tanks for them to use in attacking and confusing Allied troops from behind their own lines."

"The ultimate bad guy," Baghdadi remarked.

"That's so. But he knew where a lot of bodies were buried. After the War, the Soviet Union got into a forty-year pissing contest with its former allies. Each side tried to use its own 'former' Nazis. Skorzeny escaped prosecution with the help of the American O.S.S., which subsequently became the C.I.A."

"What does this have to do with me, Mister Caen?"

"Israel achieved its independence in 1948. None of its neighbors were very happy with that. Nasser of Egypt in particular. He recruited a bunch of former Nazi scientists to develop a missile program designed to wipe Israel off the map. Without going into any detail, Israeli intelligence 'enlisted' Otto Skorzeny to get rid of the German scientists and Egypt's efforts collapsed, as did Nasser, soon after."

"Are you saying you want me to turn coat and work for the Israelis? Rat out my own people?"

"Your own people?"

"The Islamic world."

"Not the Islamic State?"

"Not anymore," the former Caliph replied sadly.

"You'll notice how never-ending their loyalty was to you."

"But that's not everyone."

"Of course not. The vast majority, the foot soldiers, were, like most of the world, sheep who were led around by the most powerful voice. Do you truly believe they didn't defect to the next strong leader to come along and lead them to feel they were part of something larger?"

"I don't know what to say."

"Abu, most Muslims, for that matter most Jews, Christians, Buddhists, whatever you want to call then, simply want to live their lives as quietly and peacefully as they can, not disturbing anyone and not wanting to be disturbed. In that respect, a human being is not that much different from a hamster. You know, those little animals that live most of their lives in a cage and run around happily inside a revolving wheel. They feel comfortable within their limits, not horribly challenged by anything except where the next meal is coming from, and they're content."

"But our Movement could have taught the world a better life."

"Abu, how many came to your call? Really?"

"Hundreds of thousands."

"Fifty thousand?"

"Maybe."

"Out of seven *billion*?"

"What is it you propose?"

"Nothing as clandestine or exciting as you seem to think. Nothing that isn't already done between Israel and its 'enemies,' the Saudis, the Jordanians, the Egyptians, the Turks, even the Iranians."

"Surely not the Iranians, who've vowed to destroy the Little Satan?"

"Don't be too sure. You met Mister Tabrizi?"

"Yes ..."

"There are hundreds, maybe thousands more like him than you think. Or does the world forget so soon that only a few years ago our folks cooperated with the Iranians to save the Supreme Leader. I'm simply suggesting that you've had a life of glory and a bellyful of war. Maybe it's time you did what the lady in the GPS says, 'recalculate' and redirect your heart and mind toward helping the family of nations come together. After all, when people finally did come together they managed to defeat your Movement."

"What do your people want me to do? Kill? Destroy? Spy?"

"Nothing that dramatic, Abu al-Baghdadi. Simply keep your eyes and ears open to what is going on around you. If you see anything strange or different, if you see unusual activity on the part of those outside the community of nations, al-Qaeda, Taliban, they go by many names and ideologies, just let us know. Many years ago, an American, Benjamin Franklin, said, 'A stitch in time saves nine.' It's much easier to combat a disease if you catch it early enough."

"There's wisdom in what you say, Ezra Caen. I'll need some time to think it over."

"That's all I ask, Abu al-Baghdadi. That's all anyone can ask. Where do you go from here?"

"Back into obscurity. Somewhere between here and there. Do you really expect me to go into more detail?"

"Not really. *Salaam aleikum*, my friend. I wish you peace."

"And I you, Ezra Caen. *Shalom Aleichem.*"

Thus it was that the two men parted, one to the East, one to the South. And thus it was that the Wrecking Crew passed into history.

# *Epilogue:*
# *Ten Years Later*

"He made it to ninety-four. Helluva good run, and he died happy. It might be an awfully sacrilegious statement for me to make at Tommy's Memorial Service, but he still had all of his marbles when he passed."

Pedro tried to suppress a laugh, but lost his battle with dignity and guffawed. When he had regained his self-control, he said, "That's true, Sister, thanks in large part to you. Let's hope you'll still be dancing at ninety-four."

"Yeah, right, in a wheelchair or a walker. In case you hadn't noticed, I've become a little portly in the past decade."

"Finally retired, did you?"

"Yep. To Chicago in the summer and Palm Beach in the winter. My only complaint is what doesn't hurt doesn't work anymore. Getting old is not for sissies. Still, it makes me feel so much younger to see so many of our comrades-in-arms at this 'do.' Ezra, Dennis, Manucher, the Avelinos. Then there's the new generation …"

"For sure. Who'd have thought I'd ever be where I am today? Two strikes against me, couldn't get a job, going down a slide to nowhere at ninety miles an hour … Oh, Jeeze, here comes that walking mouth. Lord protect us all."

"Don't give me that 'Holier than thou' sh-, er, stuff, I'm sorry Sister Maureen," the shorter man said, blushing.

"No need to apologize Chuey, or do you prefer 'Jesus' now, although I do find your nametag 'El Gerente' to be a bit pretentious?" the former Field Marshal said, grinning broadly. "On the other hand, you were instrumental in getting our new Congressman elected. What did our Pedro have to bribe you with? Women? Money?"

"Neither," Garza said huffily. "It's honor enough to be the Congressman's aide, in charge of his tri-county office. Of course, being married to Hizzoner's wife's hairdresser isn't too hard to take, since Rosalinda will get the good gossip before anyone else does. And when it's time for him to run for Senator in a few years …"

"Okay, my courageous comrades in arms," Pedro said. "Time for us to sing one last song in honor of the departed."

As they started to sing *It's a Wonderful World*, Sister Maureen stopped them in mid-sentence. "I don't think that's quite what Tommy 'Legs' would have wanted as his swan song."

"What then?" Pedro asked.

"Well…" Sister Maureen said, a bright gleam in her eye. "The song they sang on that day when the Islamic State started to fall apart." She nodded knowingly at the band, which picked up the anthem while the room burst out:

> "Young man, there's no need to feel down, I said
> Young man, pick yourself off the ground, I said
> Young man, 'cause you're in a new town
> There's no need … to … be … unhappy
> Young man, there's a place you can go, I said
> Young man, when you're short on your dough, You can

Stay there … and I'm sure you will find
Many ways … to … have … a good time . . . . . It's fun to stay at the
**Y.M.C.A. …. Y.M.C.A.**
They have everything there for you men to enjoy
You can hang out with all the boys …
LA, LA, LA-LA ….. LA, LA, LA-LA ….."

# THE END

## *My thanks to ...*

I'm frequently asked, "How long does it take you to write a novel?" and "How many hours a day do you write?" Without in any way meaning to sound snide or "Holier than Thou," the real answer is elusive and differs with every book I write.

In answer to the first question, *Standoff* took just under three weeks to write. *Legacy*, my first effort, went through thirty-four rewrites and took nearly two years from start to finish. Well, that's a bit of a lie ... the original concept for the book, along with the first foreword, which ultimately became the final chapter, came to me in 1971, the year after I returned from living in Turkey for two years. But life is what gets in the way when you're planning something else, and, like so many first-time writers, the concept remained dormant for many years, until 1989, when I finally started to write ... and shortly thereafter realized how little I knew about the craft. Gary Jennings, the late, great novelist, whose *Aztec* became a worldwide best seller, and whose *Spangle*, which I consider one of the finest novels ever written, but which did abysmally poorly in sales, was my teacher, mentor, and friend, who taught me so much about the art of historical fiction. Although it is impossible for me to remotely project an "average" of how long it takes me to write a novel, if I had to be pinned down, I'd say between three and eight months and that's *after* I start writing. For example, this book took 4½ months to write, but I had gone through three different ideas for novels and had started all three over a period of ten months before I concluded, "This is the one."

The second question is easier to answer, because I've developed a habit pattern over the years. By nature, I consider myself an incredibly lazy person. For the first two months of any book I start, I'll write for two hours on a Saturday morning and two hours on a Sunday morning. About that time, the book starts to write itself – I swear that's the truth – and after dinner Lorraine is usually talking to parents or preparing for the next day or week at the school where she's been teaching for the past 28 years. She's on one side of the table, I'm on the other, and it's not yet time to go to bed, so … I figure I'll get an hour, maybe an hour-and-a-half of writing – and then the book really starts to move along. No "long-suffering author" stuff for me. Being a full-time trial lawyer, playing piano to accompany third grade productions, being a daddy and now a "Pop-Pop," and being married to the most wonderful woman in the world is more than enough blessings for me.

One thing is a constant: I've had friends, relatives, my writer's group, and so many people helping me along the way. Some of them don't even know how helpful they've been – often they show up as characters in my novels. But for this one, among "the usual suspects" and among those who show up only occasionally, I really do want to thank…

The members of my writing group, some of whom have shared joys, sorrows, and, of course, rejections, for twenty-five years: Paul Karrer, Joyce Krieg, Dennis Alexander, Bill Daniels, Anne Canright, Leslie Penley, Arlen Grossman, Walter Gourlay, who passed away at 94, and, most recently, Tom Burns, who left us way too soon; P.D. Cacek, a treasured member of an earlier writer's group, who has remained my close friend; and Laurie Harper, the loveliest literary agent, guide, and true professional, in the business.

The publisher, editors, designers, and geniuses in Israel, Austria, Germany, the United States, and Australia, who, since 2005, have been my team on every book I write: Zvi Morik, Director of Dekel Publishing House (Israel), Samuel Wachtman's Sons (U.S.), and Lindenfels von Pressel Verlag (Germany), who more than made good on his promises to me when I first joined Dekel, to treat me like the franchise – a helluva lot better than the big houses; Lisa Peaks, the most brilliant book designer in the universe; Pnina Ophir, Dory Morik, Katie Roman, Steve Beneš, and Peter Evans, who've been wonderful editors, advisors, friends, and critics, and who have put up with a "wild card" like me for so many years.

Thanks to Fakhri Bsoul., Ph.D, for his invaluable scholarly assistance concerning Arabic language and culture.

Closer to home: Barry and Seung Dolowich, Andy and Kiane Swartz, Calvin and Lila Seldin, Tony Seton, Michele and Howard Morton, Margie and Jack Lotz, Cathy Turkell, Erle and Patty MacDonald, and Jayson Elliott, wonderful companions on this road of life; Jean and Birgit Mouton – "the Sheep and Sheep Madame," and Al Fasulo, "the proper copper," entertaining neighbors who could serve as truly "fun" characters in any book! Sarah Cavassa, who combines beauty, brains, and incredible legal talent in a marvelous human being, her equally bright husband, Steve Beneš, Alex "Cooper" Kirkwood; Doctors Howard Oriba, Jerry Rubin, Michael Klassen and Danny Kirby; Courtney Hamilton, Cathy Turkell, Phillip Belushi, Beth Piña, and Larry Biegel; Joyce Krieg told me, "You'd better find a kickass female lead character for this book!" I couldn't have done better as a model than the real Maureen Richards and her husband, retired surgeon "Gentle Ben" Richards. And yes, Richard and Maria Avelino *do* exist exactly as portrayed in this novel. Jacob S. Lo and Alisa Fineman, friends, and extraordinary human beings.

Still closer to the center of my universe: Dick and Claire Gorman, my closest friends for more than 50 years; Herb and Sharon Chelner, Bob Mueller, Colleen Miller, my daytime "everything" for the past 30 years: paralegal, office manager, mommy, confidante, editor, "keep me in line or throw me under the bus" friend, and, of course, her loving husband, "Our Will." My "little brother" Ted, his wife Candy, their children and grandchildren; my "baby sister," Margie, her husband Harmon, their children and grandchildren. Lorraine's brother, Harry Klompas, his wife Margie, their children and grandchildren; our own children, Jeff, Tracy, Greg, Karen, and Roslyn; and our grandchildren, Jake, Abby, Ryland, Oliver, Fineas, and Vivian.

And, finally, the very reason for my existence,<br>
the core of my happiness, and,<br>
God willing, my partner throughout eternity, my Lorraine.

I thank and bless you all.

Hugo N. Gerstl
Monterey, CA. Dec. 2016

Made in the USA
Charleston, SC
07 January 2017